SHOOT

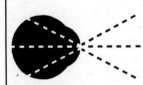

A VALENTINO MYSTERY

SHOOT

LOREN D. ESTLEMAN

THORNDIKE PRESS
A part of Gale, Cengage Learning

GALE
CENGAGE Learning·

Farmington Hills, Mich • San Francisco • New York • Waterville, Maine
Meriden, Conn • Mason, Ohio • Chicago

GALE
CENGAGE Learning®

LIBRARY OF CONGRESS CATALOGING-IN-PUBLICATION DATA

Names: Estleman, Loren D., author.
Title: Shoot : a Valentino mystery / by Loren D. Estleman.
Description: Large print edition. | Waterville, Maine : Thorndike Press, 2016. |
   ©2016 | Series: Thorndike Press large print mystery
Identifiers: LCCN 2016014183| ISBN 9781410490889 (hardcover) | ISBN 1410490882
   (hardcover)
Subjects: LCSH: Large type books. | GSAFD: Mystery fiction.
Classification: LCC PS3555.S84 S49 2016b | DDC 813/.54—dc23
LC record available at http://lccn.loc.gov/2016014183

Published in 2016 by arrangement with St. Martin's Press, LLC

Printed in Mexico
3 4 5 6 7 8 20 19 18 17 16

To Charlotte Sherman, with love;
and
to Rex Allen, Michael Ansara,
Gene Autry, William Boyd,
Johnny Mack Brown, Leo Carrillo,
Sunset Carson, Wild Bill Elliott, Dale
Evans, Kirby Grant, Tim Holt,
Lash LaRue, Ken Maynard,
Tim McCoy, Clayton Moore,
Duncan Renaldo, Tex Ritter,
Roy Rogers, Gail Russell,
Jay Silverheels, Bob Steele,
Guy Williams,
and all the others who
won the West every Saturday

I like westerns. I don't know what they have to do with anything, but I like 'em.

— Robert Redford, *Havana*

■ ■ ■ ■

I
HORSE OPERA

■ ■ ■ ■

1

"This is cute." Harriet Johansen touched a sample.

"Cute isn't what we're going for," Valentino said.

She smiled, a bit stiffly. "Pardon me, maestro."

They were seated beside Leo Kalishnikov, Valentino's architect and designer, at a large table in a studio in Tarzana — the only city in the United States named after a fictional character — browsing through a heavy volume the size of a family photo album. The studio was on the third floor of a faux-Spanish modern house with stucco walls and enormous Plexiglas windows overlooking the residential sprawl, with natural light flooding in; a shoreward-bound wind had exiled the smog into the desert east of L.A., where presumably it shriveled away in the Mojave heat.

The house was so well-proportioned that

11

from a distance it looked no larger than the average McMansion, but it covered a city block.

"It's an exact copy of Harold Lloyd's estate in Beverly Hills," said their hostess, a tall woman hovering around fifty in black leotards and tights with her hair cut short and dyed glossy Florsheim-black. Valentino thought she looked like a retired ballerina from some Eastern Bloc country; the fact that she spoke with no accent at all confirmed her foreignness.

It was a bright, airy space, a thousand square feet of terracotta tiles, eggshell-colored paneling, lighting both indirect and direct, original architects' drawings in copper frames on the walls, and bolts of material lined up in racks like torpedoes waiting to be loaded.

But in place of pages of photographs, the huge book contained carpet samples. The one Harriet had pointed out was a brightly colored image of film reels uncoiling serpentine strips of celluloid in yellow on a burgundy background.

"Indeed," said Kalishnikov. "We're designing a classic motion-picture palace, not a home theater for the basement of a used-car baron in the Valley."

Harriet looked at him. She was uncommonly pretty in casual dress, a fitted shirt with the tail out over Capri pants and the cuffs turned back, her ash-blond hair in a ponytail tied with a blue bandanna. "Isn't that what *you* do when you're not designing motion-picture palaces?"

He said nothing. He wore his favorite working uniform of silk-lined opera cape over a cutaway coat. His broad-brimmed gaucho hat lay on a corner of the table. Shiny patches of grafted skin pulled his seventy-year-old eyes into an Asian tilt. So far he'd neither spoken to Harriet nor even looked her way. Plainly he resented an outsider's intrusion into the appointment.

Valentino, hoping to defuse the tension, asked their hostess standing on the other side of the table how many more books she had in stock.

"Let's see." She glanced at the stack of books they'd discarded. "You've been through sixteen. There are twenty-four left."

"I meant of *theater* carpet."

"Yes, I know."

He groaned inwardly. The whole thing was uncomfortably like evaluating samples of wedding invitations, an ordeal he'd been unaware of until a close friend who was going through that actual process had related it to him in excruciating detail. He loved

Harriet, but he wasn't ready for that plunge. The years he'd already invested in restoring The Oracle to its Prohibition-era glory was challenge enough for now.

He turned to the architect. "What about that one with the Greek letters?"

"You mean the Arabesque." Kalishnikov, who seemed to have a photographic memory for which sample was in which book, off-loaded four volumes from the towering stack of deadwood, dragged over one bound in aubergine vinyl, and opened it directly to the sample. The squarish design, resembling hieroglyphics, was a border in muted gold on a midnight-blue background; the fibers were stiff, made of some synthetic material that resembled wool but were guaranteed to withstand ten years of heavy foot-traffic. From an inside breast pocket he drew a flat wallet, the kind made to contain square foreign currency, and slid out a photograph. It was black-and-white, a digital copy of an old snapshot taken of The Oracle sometime during the Great Depression. "Drapes, please, Sila. It will never be seen under natural illumination."

The woman nodded and touched something under the table. Blackout curtains glided noiselessly across the windows, suspended from a hidden track.

14

"Dimmers, please. I'll tell you when it's right."

She touched something else. Slowly the light in the room softened. This went on until Valentino could barely make out his companions' faces.

"Spasibo."

Sila immediately halted the dimming process; which settled the question of her origins, so far as he was concerned. Kalishnikov had fled Belarus shortly after the USSR fell.

For a time he studied the sample as it would appear in a room lit only by wall sconces and stumble-bulbs on aisle risers.

"We can't be sure about the colors, of course," he said, "but the pattern is similar."

Valentino and Harriet watched him closely, their heads almost touching, her hand gripping his under the table, tightly enough to compress his knuckles. He felt a ghost of a promise of the dawn of hope.

Kalishnikov shook his head. Hope flickered, died.

He closed the book, returned the photo to the wallet, the wallet to the pocket, and the book to the stack. "Similar is not the same."

The film archivist winced; Harriet was a CSI with the L.A.P.D., and years of working with forceps and rib-spreaders had given

15

her the grip of the daring young woman on the flying trapeze. "At exactly what point did I lose control of this project I'm paying for?" he asked Kalishnikov.

"When you signed the contract. You agreed to respect my decisions. 'I want this done right, or not at all.' Your exact words when you called me; I remind you I was in Venice at the time, installing a screening room for a film director with the government arts program in Rome. I equate 'right' with 'authentic,' yes?"

He acknowledged defeat with a nod. When Kalishnikov slipped into an immigrant's use of English, the battle was over. Harriet, sensitive as always to Valentino's every mood, relaxed her grasp and patted his hand.

The architect drew a platinum watch from a vest pocket and popped open the lid. A tiny hidden music box played "Lara's Theme" from *Doctor Zhivago*. "We'll have to continue this at another time. I have to meet with a member of the Department of the Interior."

"Whatever for?" Harriet asked.

"A shipment of mahogany has come in from Central America, and I must show papers to prove that it did not come from the Brazilian rainforest. Things were so

16

much simpler when the aristocrats were allowed to rape the earth without interference." He stood, bowed to the woman who owned the decorating firm, then to Harriet, acknowledging her existence for the first time. "I bid you all good day." He groped his way out.

The lights came up, the curtains slid back into their invisible wall pockets: Intermission. Everything in Southern California seemed to have been built on the picture-palace standard.

Valentino watched the woman returning the books they'd been through to a tall shelf. He hoped she had a system of determining which ones they'd seen. The prospect of going back to scratch made Sisyphus' job look part-time.

But he was grateful for the break. They'd spent four hours staring at carpet samples. His neck was stiff, his eyes stung, his head spun with colors and patterns like a kaleidoscope gone rogue, and he still couldn't tell taupe from beige or burgundy from claret or sea- from foam-green or charcoal from chalk from iron from ash from gunmetal from — *fifty shades of gray, my* —

Harriet checked the time on her smartphone. "Just as well. We should get ready for the reception."

17

They'd descended the stairs to the foyer, whose walls were shingled with framed autographed photos of celebrity customers in glass frames. Just looking at them made him think of flocks of dollar bills sprouting wings and flying out the window. A pale female creature as sleek as the décor sat behind a glass desk. Everything on the ground floor appeared to be made of glass; even her legs looked like stemware. She didn't look up from her copy of *Elle* as they walked past.

"What reception?"

"Don't act ignorant. You know the one."

"I thought that was next week."

"No, you didn't. You see the invitation every day. I taped it to your bathroom mirror so you wouldn't forget."

"Can't we give it a pass? Trust me, nobody will notice."

"I thought you were a fan."

"I am; but you know how these affairs go. The room will be so crowded we won't be able to see anything, and we'll be lucky to have thirty seconds with the host. Anyway, it's sad. He's shutting down the museum because no one's interested in his kind of western anymore."

She patted his hand and smiled. "You're not no one, Val. I happen to know you

18

passed up an offer for your original Red Montana cap pistols that would have paid for twenty square feet of carpet for that old barn of yours."

"Not just the pistols," he said. "The guy wanted the holster, too; also the hat, vest, chaps, and boots. They'd have paid for the rest. But now the bottom will drop out of the market because every collector in the country will be after the originals. They've never been for sale before."

"You could have sold yours at any time."

"So I'm stupid. So what?"

"So you're both the last of your breed, you and Red. Trust me, he'll give you more than thirty seconds."

Which was truer than even Harriet predicted.

2

He took in his breath when Harriet opened her door. She wore a low-cut evening dress of some shimmery material that clung to her in all the best places and changed colors when she turned around for his inspection. The back was cut in a daring scoop, exposing her well-defined deltoids.

"You look like an expensive sports car," he said.

"I guess I can take that as a compliment."

"That's how it was intended. I'm in the middle of negotiations with a retired assistant director for some home movies he shot on the set of *Bullitt.* Cars get under your skin like —"

"Grease under your nails. You clean up pretty well yourself."

He touched his black silk bow tie. "I appreciate that. I rented the tux. They threw in the alterations for free, so I wasn't expecting much."

"I'm glad they included a cummerbund. When you took me to the Oscars I saw more white cloth than Grant at Appomattox."

"I had to buy that separately. Did you know it was originally called a crumberbund, because it was designed to catch crumbs when you're dining? I got that from the salesman; he said that's how you know which way the pleats go when you put it on."

She drew a filmy white scarf over her bare shoulders and picked up a tiny handbag that matched her gown. "Let's saddle up, cowboy."

The Red Montana and Dixie Day Museum was circled — like the covered wagons in one of their films — by Broadway and the Ventura, Glendale, and Golden State freeways. The building, a super-sized replica of an adobe ranch house, topped a low, green, perfect dome of a hill, with a spacious parking lot centered around a larger-than-life bronze sculpture of the cowboy star in his prime aboard a bucking bronco — Tinderbox, of course — atop a pedestal with the titles of his seventy-two films engraved on a brass plate.

A twentysomething parking valet in a yoke-front shirt and skin-tight Levi's looked doubtfully at Valentino's ten-year-old

Chevy, but gave him a claim ticket with a polite smile and slid under the wheel. The owner grasped the door before he could close it. "You might need to jiggle the wheel to get the key out of the ignition. It's cranky sometimes."

"Don't look so contrite," Harriet told him as the attendant drove off. "So it's not Steve McQueen's Mustang. A new Cadillac would cost more than those twin three-D cameras you're always talking about."

"I meant to look disdainful. Everyone in this town judges you by your wheels."

"Not everyone. I fell for your cute butt at first sight." She squeezed it surreptitiously.

Near the entrance stood another bronze — smaller than the one out front — of Dixie Day, Montana's co-star and wife of many years, looking dazzlingly beautiful in cowgirl dress, holding the reins of her mare, Cocoa.

A security guard at the door asked to see their invitation. He wore a sheriff's star and the stag handle of the revolver on his hip resembled Valentino's prized cap pistols, but that would be where the similarity ended. A walkie-talkie balanced it out on the other side. The film archivist handed him the stiff sheet of rag paper bordered with rearing horses. In serifed Wanted-poster letters it read:

YOU AND A PARD ARE INVITED TO A SHINDIG
TO
CELEBRATE SIXTY YEARS OF RIP-ROARIN'
MEMORIES ON THE
OCCASION OF THE CLOSING OF THE
RED MONTANA AND DIXIE DAY
MUSEUM
PLEASE CONSIDER KICKING IN TO THE
DIXIE DAY CANCER FOUNDATION.

The date and time were included in script resembling a curling lariat.

The guard thanked him and unhooked the rope — a real rope, made of hemp — that barred the entrance.

"I hope I don't look like a piker when I chip in what I can afford," Valentino whispered as they pushed through a pair of wooden bat-wing saloon doors. "I owe them the price of restoring the mezzanine for all the entertainment they've given me."

"They'll be grateful for whatever you can donate. From the Humvees and the Mercedeses in the parking lot, my guess is they'll bring in plenty."

"That's just it. I don't even know why I was invited. Kyle wasn't, and he's the head of the department."

"Don't sell yourself short, Val. Maybe Montana's familiar with your reputation.

23

You've uncovered more lost films than anyone else at UCLA. As for 'giving' you entertainment, they didn't build all this on a truck driver's salary."

"All this" was indeed impressive. A painting the size of a barn door greeted them inside, showing an implausibly young Montana smiling broadly astride Tinderbox under his trademark milk-white Stetson, with Dixie beside him in Cocoa's saddle. Both wore elaborately embroidered western costumes. They were aglow with health, the man tanned and handsome, the woman as stunning as when she'd represented Oklahoma in the Miss America pageant. The portrait was signed in Norman Rockwell's distinctive block-print hand.

The crowd inside sipped red and white wine from plastic goblets, conversing and admiring framed movie posters, bright splashes of red and yellow with six-guns blazing and horses plunging down steep canyons, spangled shirts, woolly chaps, and fringed skirts on form-fitted dummies in glass cases, and an arsenal of chrome-plated revolvers, gold-chased carbines, and wicked-looking bowie knives on display. Harriet, an inveterate connoisseur of women's footwear, lingered over pairs of Dixie's cowgirl boots handmade with ostrich, crocodile, and rhinoceros hides in scarlet, turquoise, emerald, pearl, and ashes-of-rose, decorated with Indian signs and tulips. Bright electric bulbs in glass oil-lamp chimneys illuminated everything from wagon wheels suspended from the ceiling. Nothing had been overlooked; even the floor beneath their feet was a tile mosaic of Montana and Day backed by Old Glory.

"I like this one best of all," said Harriet, as they stood before a simple black-and-white photo in a silver frame of the cowboy actor in western-cut formalwear and his brand-new bride in a conventional wedding dress with a white veil. "They look as happy as any two kids starting their lives together."

Valentino, hoping that wasn't a hint, read the engraving on the small brass rectangle set into the base of the frame:

Mr. and Mrs. Lionel Phelps
June 25th, 1956

"He never did change his name legally," Valentino said. "I forget what Dixie's is in real life."

"Agnes," said a voice behind them. "Somehow I don't think 'Lionel Phelps and Agnes Mulvaney, King and Queen of the West' would of sold many tickets."

They turned to face their host. Despite the two-inch heels on his glossy boots, Red Montana in person was not as tall as he appeared on-screen, and he'd put on weight since retirement; his chins spilled over the knot of his necktie, cutting the crown off the hat of the cowboy twirling a lasso hand-painted on silk. His suit, with flared lapels and arrow pockets, was beautifully cut, although it probably hadn't cost much more than his head of silver hair, a tribute to the wigmaker's craft. His voice was reedy with age, but retained an echo of its famous timbre: He could still have sung "Tumblin' Along with the Tumblin' Tumbleweeds" and sold it.

Valentino shook his hand; it was liver-spotted, but he had the grip of a career politician. "Good evening, Mr. Montana. I'm —"

"I know who you are, son. All the invites are numbered, and the lawman at the door keeps me posted on the arrivals by that gizmo he wears on his belt. Who's the pretty filly you brung along?"

"This is my friend, Harriet Johansen."

He beamed all over and took her hand as delicately as if it were made of thin crystal. "How'd'ya do? I'm obliged to you both for coming." He turned toward the wedding

26

photo. "I picked that date on account of it was the hundredth anniversary of Custer's Last Stand. It was a Monday, so we done it after dark. Wouldn't do for the world's biggest western stars to get hitched in front of a bunch of empty seats on account of work."

"How did Mrs. Phelps feel about marrying on the day of a cavalry defeat?" Harriet asked.

"Fine and dandy. That little lady shot an arrow straight through my heart."

"Good answer!"

"Thank you for having us, Mr. —" Valentino hovered between "Montana" and "Phelps."

"Red, son. You wouldn't know it to look at the snow on this old roof, but folks've been calling me that since a long time before I knew a camera from a dry wash." He looked at the Rolex on his wrist, a custom-made one with his own image aboard a rearing horse on the dial. "I got to get ready to make a speech, but I'd be obliged if you'd see me in the curator's office afterwards." He patted him on the shoulder and moved off, wringing hands on his way through the crowd.

"You see?" Harriet said. "Your reputation precedes you."

They paused to admire a Concord stagecoach, which the plaque on the stand erected in front of it assured them was an original, acquired from the Butterfield line by Montana himself and a feature in every one of his films from *Sunrise Over Texas* through *Song of San Antonio,* then entered the gift shop.

There were reproductions on sale of the original posters in the museum, action figures of Red Montana, Dixie Day, Sam "Slap" O'Reilly, Red's sidekick and source of most of the series' comic relief, DVDs of all the stars' surviving movies, coloring books, Montana's "as told to" autobiography, a glossy coffee-table book, *The Films of Red Montana,* a cookbook, *Dixie Day's Authentic Ranch Recipes,* cap pistols, movie stills, and miniature copies, in bronze or resin (depending upon one's budget), of the colossal statues in front of the museum. An authentic-looking wooden cigar store Indian, grimly grasping a fistful of cigars and scratched all over by generations of matches, occupied a corner with a sign at its feet informing customers that it was not for sale. A pretty salesgirl in a blouse embroidered with cactus flowers and a fringed skirt smiled vapidly behind a glass counter filled with watches, bracelets, necklaces, and money clips, all adorned with images of

"The Sweethearts of the West," complete with a *TM* at the end of the phrase on the sign advertising them.

"There's gold in them thar hills," Harriet said.

"Chickenfeed. Red owns a Mexican soccer team, the Acapulco Piranhas, with a private suite built into a brand-new stadium, just as a hobby. They made it into the World Cup Finals last year. He and Dixie own houses in Beverly Hills and Ireland, a condo on Fifth Avenue in New York, a fleet of yachts —"

"And Dixie herself?"

"Oh, she skates along: her own clothing line in all the Walmarts west of the Mississippi, a school for the blind in Oregon — she had a brother born without sight — and a quarter mile of Rodeo Drive."

"My God! I always heard the studios paid their contract players next to nothing in those days."

"Twenty-five bucks a week, for Red," he said, "fifteen to Dixie, and all they could eat at the commissary. She got that trim figure being chased around the casting couch."

"Why do I see a history lesson coming?"

3

"Red had to go on strike to get Republic to give him a trailer to change in," Valentino said. "Until then he had to show up in costume at the crack of dawn and work nonstop, sometimes until past midnight. The suits caved, but they added the days he spent off work to the time on his contract. That was standard operating procedure."

"It sounds like slavery."

"That's what the Supreme Court ruled, in the case of *De Havilland versus Warner Brothers.*"

"*Olivia* de Havilland, from *Gone with the Wind?*"

"The same. She broke the old studio system, and lost work on account of it. But whenever Kevin Costner picks a part to his liking and decides who'll direct and who'll co-star, he has Olivia to thank."

"So the studio gave Red a big fat raise."

"No, it just dropped the extension clause.

When box office receipts began to fall off and Republic didn't renew his contract, he bought up the prints of all his films; went into hock to obtain them, and everyone said he was loony. Remember, this was back when re-releases were rare. Few theaters would book a film after it had its run. But the people who laughed at him overlooked one thing."

"Television."

"Bingo. He had the prints cut up into thirty-minute episodes, syndicated them throughout the U.S., and rode the investment into multimillionaire country. At the time it made him the wealthiest actor in history. Dixie probably bought that piece of Rodeo Drive on her husband's advice. Those old cowboys knew the value of land. Back then you could have bought up half the Valley for the price of a custom-made Rolls-Royce; which Red had one of, with steer horns on the bonnet and a horn that played 'Friendly Camping on the Owl-Hoot Trail.' That was the song —"

"The song he sang with Dixie at the end of every episode of *Red Montana's Frontier Theater*. I've heard you sing it in the shower."

He was about to say, "Okay, so I'm a geek," when a piping voice interrupted him:

" 'Friendly camping on the Owl-Hoot Trail, there's no place so good; fryin' bacon on the old campfire, made from hick'ry wood! Friends, there's just no substitute, no buried gold will do; friendly camping on the Owl-Hoot Trail —"

"— just me and you,' " Valentino finished, smiling at the little boy who'd sung to him. He was about five years old, decked out in the complete Montana kit: white hat with a broad curved brim, red suede vest, yoke-front shirt, riveted jeans, red boots, and a genuine Red Montana gun belt with a cap pistol on each hip. He was a mass of freckles and sure-enough red hair, missing a front tooth.

A man wearing the same hair color took a long step, scooping the boy off the floor. "I'm sorry if he bothered you. We've shown him all of Red's shows on DVD since he learned to walk. All the other parents were bombarding their kids with Mozart, but we thought —"

"Don't apologize," Valentino said. "I've got nothing against classical music, but most of what I know about honorable behavior I learned growing up with Red's reruns on Nick at Nite; my father saw them the first time around every Saturday morning."

A woman joined them. She was about the same age as the man, an attractive redhead an inch or two taller than him in a simple black cocktail dress with spaghetti straps on her square shoulders. Her companion wore a white dinner jacket, patently better fitted to his frame than Valentino's rental. But something about them, apart from the ornamentation, exuded money.

"I couldn't help overhearing you," she said. "We're bringing up little Jack to respect the values of the mid-twentieth century. Most of what our parents learned about manners they got from *their* parents, the Depression and World War Two generation, and television programs like *The Lone Ranger* and Red Montana: gentlemanly behavior, the difference between right and wrong. I think we've gotten away from that in our society; but that doesn't mean we can't reaffirm it with the proper exposure."

Valentino was still framing a response when Harriet grasped the woman's hand. "Harriet Johansen. This tongue-tied fellow is Valentino."

"Laura Overholt. My husband, Evan."

Valentino shook both their hands. "I wasn't so much tongue-tied as in awe. To meet a young man who knows all the lyrics to 'Friendly Camping' — well, I'd thought with his generation anything that happened more than thirty seconds before his birth —"

"The theme of my book!" From a small clutch the woman brought out a card and handed it to him:

L. OVERHOLT, PH.D.

"You're writing a book?"

"*Planned Adolescence: The Rationale Behind Denying The Past, and its Effect Upon Development.* And you are — ?"

"Valentino," he reminded her. I'm an archivist with the UCLA Department of Film Preservation."

She clapped her hands like a child. "I read about you in the *Times*! You're renovating that old theater."

"And enervating myself at the same time."

Evan said, "It must be quite a challenge."

"That's an understatement. At the moment I've got my contractor combing the country for a decent wood-carver who works in mahogany. All the dadoes were done by Old World craftsmen, and between termites and dry rot half of them need replacing. But the best ones we can find are way outside my budget and the ones that aren't are busy with other projects."

34

Little Jack squirmed. His father lowered him to the floor and told him to stay put. "I may be able to help you there. I'm an attorney. My firm handles immigration cases and contract law, among others. We just won a temporary injunction against INS. Our client, Victor Stavros, was born on an American ocean-liner on the way from Greece, and some shyster told Victor Senior that made him a citizen, so the old man didn't bother to apply for his son when he himself was naturalized. It took Washington thirty years to catch up, but now they want to deport the son."

"That's terrible," Harriet said.

"I think we can iron it out. Meanwhile, the old man needs the work to cover his legal expenses. I doubt he'll gouge you. I've seen his work. He's a master cabinetmaker. You won't be disappointed."

The boy tugged at his mother's skirt. She stooped and picked him up. Valentino admired her biceps.

"Thank you!" he said. "That's the first ray of hope in a long time."

"Thank *you*. We've been hoping to put him to work. Say what you like about lawyers, we aren't all out to suck blood." Evan Overholt took a card out of a leather case, scribbled on the back of it, and gave it to Valentino. "That's my cell number. I'll put you in contact. Meanwhile, maybe we can all get together for dinner sometime."

"We'd like that," Harriet said, before Valentino could reply.

Throughout their visit, the legendary country band known as the Texas Wranglers had been playing a medley of Red Montana's songs in the museum's main room. Now the lead guitar plucked out a string version of the bugled opening of a horse race. The host was about to make his speech. The browsers in the gift shop began to move in that direction.

Harriet took Valentino's arm. "I feel good about this. Kyle and Fanta are the only couple we know socially. They're good company, but we need variety."

"It's fine with me. I'm just glad we don't have to reproduce those dadoes in plastic. Leo'd throw a fit."

The crowd had gathered in front of a dais at the far end of the room, where the Wranglers stood idly holding their instruments behind Red Montana. Beside it — a humorous touch — stood an authentic-looking rustic outhouse, complete with slant roof and half-moon cut in the door. It was padlocked, and a sign politely invited attendees to poke their checks and cash

36

through the half-moon on behalf of the Dixie Day Foundation. Harriet and Valentino had each contributed a check made out in the amount of fifty dollars, which was as much as they could afford.

The microphone squealed. The man in the tailored western suit adjusted it, tapped it, and got a satisfying *thump-thump-thump* in response. He coughed into his fist, cleared his throat.

"Howdy, friends and neighbors. I ain't tall on speechifyin', so I'll make this short and sweet. I'm sorry to tell you that the Red Montana and Dixie Day Museum is headed for the last round-up."

A collective "Ohhhhhh" rose from the crowd. The news that the institution was closing its doors wasn't new, but Valentino guessed from the response he wasn't the only one who'd been hoping for a reprieve.

"Me, too," Montana said, and more quietly, "Me, too. But even the frontier couldn't live forever. Folks these days like their westerns gritty and violent. As most of you know, in seventy-two pictures I never killed a single person, not counting an assistant director or two."

The audience laughed.

"No, I winged 'em, roped 'em, wrassled 'em, and punched 'em in the jaw, but I always stopped short of mortal bloodshed, on account of —"

" 'A man who'd take another man's life is no man a-tall,' " chimed in a number of voices.

"Thank you kindly. I only wisht there was a hundred times more of you who know my movies by heart, to help pay for the upkeep. Next week, a crew will be here to haul all this stuff to New York City and put it up for auction, even this ole hoss of mine." He stepped to the edge of the dais and smacked Tinderbox on his muscular flank, where he stood rampant on a pedestal, pawing the air with his gold-shod hooves. Valentino paid close attention, but he couldn't tell from the sound if the rumor was true that Montana had arranged for "The Most Famous Stallion in the World" to be skinned and stuffed after death. (The running tasteless joke was that Dixie Day feared the same fate.) The actor himself was famously mum on the subject. "That way, all of you fine folks will get a shot at taking home a little piece of old Red; so maybe this ain't so unhappy of an occasion after all.

"But just to pour a little more molasses on this flapjack, I'm pleased as punch to announce that as of this morning, the Dixie Day Foundation has raised almost two million dollars for cancer research. I expect we'll round that off when we count what's in that there prairie powder room."

The crowd cheered and applauded loudly.

"Dixie ain't feeling up to joining us tonight, but she asked me special to thank all you folks for opening up your hearts and your pocketbooks."

The reaction this time was subdued. From the moment the couple had called a press conference to inform the world that Dixie was terminally ill, tributes had been pouring in from all over the world, including those thirty-six countries where their films had been dubbed into foreign languages.

Camera flashes lit up the retired actor, who raised his arms and issued a mock-stern order not to be bashful about "bellyin' up to the chuckwagon," and stepped down to a thunder of palms.

He walked directly to where Valentino stood with Harriet. In a low voice, he said, "For chrissake, let's go in the office and take a snort. I ain't had a drop of likker since breakfast."

4

Their host smiled, showing off his expensive dentures, took Harriet's hand again and kissed it. She flushed a little; he retained most of his good looks and his charm was legendary.

"I need to talk to your beau in private," he said. "I'd take it as a favor if you'd pick out something from the jewelry counter in the gift shop as a sign you won't think bad of ole Red."

"Thank you so much, but it's unnecessary."

"Don't insult me, now. I'll be checking you out before you leave, and if you don't got on something pretty you didn't come in with, I'll take it hard."

She thanked him again and turned toward the shop.

It was obvious the office actually belonged to Montana, to be used by the curator only when his employer was absent. The walls were plastered with autographed pictures of the cowboy star shaking hands with various presidents, Ernest Hemingway, and Albert Einstein; one presented him riding horseback alongside Margaret Thatcher. His famous silver-studded saddle perched on a stand behind a desk supporting a computer console and a fax machine. His visitor recognized the desk itself as a Thomas C. Molesworth original, with a buckskin top secured with brass tacks and bowlegged ranch hands in silhouette on the front panel.

A Bierstadt landscape slid out of sight at the flip of a switch, exposing a completely furnished bar. The old man pulled the stopper from a cut-crystal decanter and filled a glass. "What's your pleasure, son? I got everything but tequila. I got sick on it shooting *Cucaracha Cowpoke* down in Sonora and can't stand the sight of it."

"Nothing, thanks."

Montana lowered himself into an enormous swivel chair upholstered in what appeared to be buffalo hide and waved Valentino into a smaller version on the other side of the desk. He took a long pull from his glass and said, "Ah!" Then he began signing eight-by-ten glossy photographs in a stack in front of him.

"Thank you again for the invitation, sir.

I've been here before, of course, but I always see something new."

"That's because there always *is* something new. Come back sometime and I'll take you and your lady friend on a tour of the storage room. You can pick up a lot of truck in sixty years in show business. I owe it all to Tinderbox. You know, when I braced the head of the studio on the subject of the pissant salary they paid, he said he'd just put me on suspension and stick someone else on the horse. 'That bag of bones is the real star,' he said. What he didn't know was that bag of bones belonged to me. I spent a year's pay on the bill of sale. Best moment I ever had in this business was when I drew it like a hogleg and waved it under his nose."

He finished signing the stack and picked up his drink. "I reckon you're curious as to why I asked you back here."

"I didn't expect to be invited at all."

"I collect business cards the way a crazy old lady collects cats. They just keep winding up on my front porch. I don't even remember how I came into this one." He drained his glass, set it down with a thump, drew a small rectangle from the top drawer of the desk, and skidded it across the top. It read:

The card included his business and contact numbers.

"I Googled your name when I came across it," Montana said, "talked to some people. They tell me you can sniff out a foot of silver nitrate stock in a pile of horse manure."

"I hope I'll never have to, but I've found portions of lost classics in places almost as unlikely."

"I need somebody with detective skills. I'd go to a pro, but I've been in the movie business sixty years. I only trust film people. I hear you can keep a secret."

"It's important if I'm going to stay ahead of billionaire entrepreneurs like Mark David Turkus." The owner and CEO of Supernova International had beaten him out of more acquisitions than he cared to remember.

"Good. What I got in mind won't stand a motormouth like one of Slap O'Reilly's old-coot prospectors. This is one secret you better start keeping right now."

"Yes, sir."

"Red. I never got past sergeant in the army."

"Red. I promise."

Montana produced a key ring with a silver horse's head attached, unlocked another drawer, and took out a nine-by-twelve manila envelope. "You know my wife is dying."

"Yes, sir; Red. I'm very sorry."

"I don't know what I'll do without her. She was my sweetheart long before she was the Sweetheart of the Range. But I'll have time enough to be sad about it later. These were faxed to me last week." He opened the envelope and handed him a sheaf of paper.

It was plain fax stock. The images that had been scanned onto the sheets were smudged and grainy, but they shocked the film archivist to his heels. He recognized Dixie Day's face from her movies. She appeared no older than twenty, naked in the arms of an unclothed anonymous male. He raised his eyes to meet the cowboy star's stony expression.

"Are you sure they're genuine?"

"I checked that out years ago, the first time I saw them. They're enlargements of frames from a stag film Dixie made before she broke in at Republic. She was plain Agnes Mulvaney then. She told me all about it the day before our wedding. She only made the one picture, to pay for an operation for her mother. I come within a hog's bristle of breaking it off right then; but I loved her. I still do, which is why I paid a hundred thousand cash for the negative and what I was told was every existing print and burned them. I figured that was the end of it until these showed up."

"You can never be sure how many prints were made. Whoever's behind this may even have made another negative from a positive. He could go on bleeding you for years. Do you think it's the same blackmailer?" He gave back the pictures.

"I don't have a clue. I put the cash in a paper sack in a locker at LAX like I was told in the letter that came with the sample print. The next day the negative and prints came by special delivery. I never made direct contact with anyone. This time I haven't even received a demand. Just these." He jammed the sheaf back into the envelope and relocked it in the drawer. "The way I see it, he wants to sweat me a little before he names his terms, so I don't try to haggle."

"That's a reasonable assumption, but why are you telling me this?"

"Why do you think? I want you to find out who sent them."

"I wouldn't know where to start."

"Talk to Sam. He's living at the Actors' Home."

"Sam?"

"Well, you know him better as Slap."

"Your old sidekick? I thought he died."

"He pretty much did, so far as the studios was concerned: drank himself right out of paying work. He's always blamed me for not going to bat for him. Drunks are never responsible for the jackrabbit holes they step in. It'd be just like him to try and get back at me by ruining Dixie's reputation. Somehow he heard about that dirty picture and got ahold of it. Maybe it was him squoze me the first time and he spent the last buck on a bottle of busthead whiskey."

"Why don't you talk to him yourself?"

"He hates my guts, that's why. He'd jack up the price just to see the look on my face."

"But why me? You've offered to match every dollar the foundation brings in. That means you can afford to hire a private agency and pay for its discretion."

"I told you I only trust film people."

"I'd like to help you, but this is way out of my league." Not to say profoundly unpleasant.

"Switch off that light, will you, son?"

Mystified, Valentino got up and flipped the switch next to the door, plunging the

46

room into gloom. At the same moment, Montana pressed something under the desk. A white screen hummed down from the ceiling and another wall decoration behind the desk, this one a reproduction of Custer's Last Stand, slid out of sight, exposing a motion-picture projector. Montana pressed something else and the projector came on with a whir.

His guest spent the next five minutes entranced by black-and-white images of galloping horses and smoking six-guns, accompanied by a tinny soundtrack full of thunderous music and hard-bitten frontier dialogue. He recognized a Red Montana younger than any he'd seen, years younger than himself, and a breathtakingly beautiful Dixie Day, who according to Hollywood lore had only that one scene.

The projector shut off abruptly, the phantoms fading from the screen. He blinked. It took him a moment to find the light switch.

"*Sixgun Sonata,*" he said. "Your first picture with Dixie."

"That was Buck Billingsley's only directing job; there was a war on in Korea, and all the house directors was shooting combat footage for the military, so he got himself hired."

"That picture's been considered lost for

decades."

"I bought it from Republic in '55 and put it in a vault. It come cheap — it stunk up the box office and Billingsley never worked again. He died not long after." Montana pinched a thumb and forefinger together and put them to his nose, sniffing. The gesture's significance wasn't lost on his guest. "I had two more pictures on my contract, and Dixie had just signed on for seven years, so the studio had to do something with us. She had a bigger part in *Wyoming Waltz,* and it was a hit. That little lady saved my bacon. Before her? *Saddle Serenade? Red River Rhapsody?* Bottom half of a double bill, and audiences was getting up and going home after the feature."

"Turkus would give you a quarter million for *Sixgun Sonata* sight unseen."

"A private collector offered me more than that last year. I told him I didn't have it. What do I need with another quarter million?"

"You could apply it to the Dixie Day Fund."

"I started that on my PR guy's advice. It's good press and keeps my name out there. I don't get no more mileage out of kicking in myself. Anyway, I had a new master struck on safety stock and destroyed the original nitrate print, so you won't have to bother with that."

"Me?"

"Your fee, payable on delivery of the blackmailer's name, O'Reilly or whoever if not him. You can do with it what you like, sell it to Turkus or give it to UCLA."

"That's incredibly generous, but I'm really not that kind of detective."

Montana sat back, resting his hands on his paunch. "The picture don't mean a thing to me. If you turn me down, I'll just burn it."

"What makes that different from blackmail?"

He offered his guest a cigar from a plain redwood box, was declined, and selected one for himself. He pierced it with a pocketknife, ignited it with a lighter with a diamond horseshoe on it, and sat back, grinning around the cigar. "I didn't say I was better than this scum. Just richer."

Valentino thought. He was reeling from the double blow of finding, then perhaps losing, a cinematic treasure and learning that this champion of the Code of the West had much in common with the bad guys he'd pursued throughout his career on the silver screen.

"I'll do it on one condition," he said then.

"You drive a hard bargain, son. What is it?"

He asked him if he'd really had Tinderbox stuffed.

5

"The young lady has taste." Gently taking Harriet's wrist, Red Montana turned it. The thin silver bracelet caught the light, drawing attention to the cluster of turquoise that decorated it. It made an attractive contrast against her tawny skin.

"I wish you'd let me pay for it," she said. "I'm afraid it wasn't the least expensive piece in the case."

"It weren't the most, either. Just do me a favor and think of ole Red when you wear it." He patted her hand and let go.

They were standing inside the entrance to the main room from the short hall leading to his office. Just then a crew from a local TV station came their way, plowing a path through the remaining guests with their cameras, sound equipment, and blinding white lights. "Stampede," said Montana with a sigh. "I promised these folks some palaver at the end of the hoedown." He took

Valentino's hand in his pulverizing grip. "Keep me posted, son. You've got my manager's number. He knows where to find me every minute of every day."

Valentino tipped the valet and joined the funerary parade waiting to leave the parking lot.

"I won't pry, since he asked to see you alone," Harriet said. "I assume he pulled an old movie out of his sleeve, a one-of-a-kind treasure of interest to the Film Preservation Department."

"That much I can confirm." He told her about *Sixgun Sonata*. "From what he showed me, it's better than audiences and critics thought at the time. I don't think they were ready for his kind of western. Now, of course, there's the nostalgia factor. We can send it around the country on the art-house circuit, then release it on DVD and Blu-ray and bump up the budget. If Kyle has any markers left, we might even swing a world premiere at Grauman's."

"It must be quite a favor he's asking."

"It's a little out of my comfort zone; but at least this time it shouldn't get me in trouble with the police."

"You sure know how to set a girl's mind at ease." She shifted in her seat, facing him with an eager expression. "Did you ask him the other thing?"

"What other thing?"

"You know." She made a whinnying noise.

"Yes; but he swore me to secrecy on that as well."

She shifted again, looking through the windshield. "You're no fun."

"Says the lady wearing the brand-new bracelet."

He got to the office earlier than usual the next morning, and was not surprised to see Ruth already seated in command position; for all he knew, the receptionist slept at her station sitting up, probably with her eyes wide open. She was at least as old as the building, the college's former power plant, but determining her true age would involve scraping off ten coats of lacquer, cutting her in two, and counting the rings.

"Ruth, get me Kym Trujillo at the Motion Picture Country Home."

She looked up from *Guns & Ammo;* he'd heard she'd decided to put in for a permit to carry a concealed weapon, which in her case struck him as overkill. "Think they'll take him?" She inclined her glossy black head of hair toward a door belonging to one of only two offices on the floor.

"I'm going to tell him you said that."

She put down the magazine and picked up her phone, displaying elaborate indifference.

"I'll take it in Dr. Broadhead's office."

Kyle Broadhead, the head of UCLA's Film Preservation Department, bawled out an invitation at Valentino's knock. He found the professor seated in his spartan office, not at his desk with its massive ludicrously obsolete computer, but on an exercise bike. Equally ludicrous was his workout costume: white shirtsleeves, necktie, gabardine slacks, and penny loafers. His shaggy dirty-gray hair glistened with perspiration, dark circles showed under his arms, and his unmade-bed of a face was distended with agony.

"Feel the burn yet?" But his visitor was alarmed. He looked like a poster boy for coronary disease.

"It's not as bad as it looks," Broadhead panted. "I take my blood pressure every fifteen minutes. The dial has yet to spin around twice and fly off. Fanta says when we walk down the aisle she wants me not to look so much like Spencer Tracy in *Father of the Bride*."

"She didn't say anything of the kind. I'm sure she just wants you to take better care of yourself."

"You're right. I got my ambition mixed

up with hers. What possessed me to propose marriage to a girl half my age?"

"Probably the same whim that possesses you to fudge the mathematics. You had two years of tenure before she was born."

"Sweet of you to point it out. How was the reception?"

"Surprising." The telephone rang. "I think that's for me."

"Help yourself. Just don't knock those papers off the desk; I'd never get them back in order. I was burning up the keys when something made a noise like a slide-whistle and it stopped numbering them."

"I'm surprised worse hasn't happened. You ought to donate that Wang to the Smithsonian." Valentino sat down at the desk and picked up the receiver.

The Motion Picture Country Home — more often referred to as the Actors' Home — was an airy, well-kept facility in Woodland Hills, supported by dues paid to the Screen Actors Guild to provide shelter and care to aging or infirm performers who might otherwise have been placed in depressing public institutions or turned out on the street if they'd failed to invest their money wisely. It was managed by Kym Trujillo, an attractive young brunette with a master's degree in Business Administration

55

who'd twice been named Administrator of the Year by the local Hispanic League.

"Good to hear from you, Val," she said. "I had my butt pinched twice this morning by a certain matinee idol."

"I can guess who. Don't judge him too harshly. That was coin of the realm back when they billed him above the title."

"I'm not complaining, really. Although I have begun to see the wisdom behind the invention of the girdle."

"Having second thoughts about the job?"

"Heaven forbid. I'm collecting research for the most devastating tell-all book in Hollywood history. Did you know John Wayne and Clara Bow were an item?"

"Everybody does; or thinks he does. The rumor is she bedded the entire USC football team when he was a linebacker, but I never bought it."

"I mean later, when he was shooting *The Big Trail* and *Wings* was in post-production. I got it as an apology for the bruise on my backside."

"Two things wrong," he said.

"Oh, God. Give it to me straight."

"One: You'll have to spend the first half of the book teaching your readers who Clara Bow was."

"You can help me out with that. I bet

56

there's an audience for a remastered video release of her films. I'll cut you in on the royalties; or your department, if you persist in your vow of poverty. Next."

"*Wings* was released in 1927; three years before *The Big Trail.* Wayne was still shooting when the first film won the first Academy Award."

"Aw, nuts. You're no fun."

"Problem with firsthand reminiscences is they always come with secondhand memories. I've gone down more blind alleys based on eyewitness accounts than Helen Keller. I need a favor."

"After dashing my hopes at the Number One slot on the *New York Times* list? Fire away."

"Do you have a guest registered under the name Sam O'Reilly? It might be Samuel, but if he used a stage name I may have to research the original."

"Sam O'Reilly. Oh, you mean Slap?"

A few gratifying minutes later, he thanked her and hung up. His gaze fell to the pile of sheets on the desk. "So you're really writing the book?" he asked Broadhead.

"Told you I had it all down up here." The professor took a hand off the handlebars to tap his bulging forehead. "The rest was paperwork."

"It's taken you only, what, twenty-five years to write a companion piece to *The Persistence of Vision*?"

"Give me a break. When nine out of ten critics — Pauline Kael, rest her soul, can kiss my newly toned behind — go on record calling your book the last word on its subject, it takes at least that long to come up with the next."

"What's the title?"

"Not sure yet. I'm thinking of something involving *Twilight.*"

"Taken."

Broadhead stopped pedaling. He mopped his face with the end of his necktie. "What's your interest in Slap O'Reilly? I'm pretty sure the board won't approve a Great Sidekicks of the West collection; disregarding the fact that either Gabby Hayes or Walter Brennan could have out-*Lear*ed Larry Olivier and Chris Plummer six ways from Tuesday."

"It's something I can't discuss."

"A sacred secret! Spill!"

"Let me substitute an ethical question: If you were offered a treasure unique to the world in return for an act that might — *might* being the operative word — bring harm to another, would you accept it?"

"No."

Valentino lifted his brows. "I didn't expect that abrupt an answer."

"Give me something harder and I'll take more time."

"What if the party who might be harmed is a criminal?"

"The thing about moral questions is the specifics are immaterial."

"What if it's a blackmailer?"

"Then I withdraw my answer."

"What happened to the specifics being immaterial?"

Broadhead dismounted. "You misstated the moral question. Anything and everything that can be done to bring harm to an extortionist is morally defensible. A murderer takes your life and that's the end of the thing. A blackmailer bleeds you little by little by little until you're as good as dead; sometimes you are dead, because he's taken away your will to survive, and we all know where that leads. Who's blackmailing Red Montana?"

"Who said anything about Red Montana?"

"The goddess of Reason. Yesterday you had no ethical dilemmas. Last night you attended a reception hosted by Montana. This morning you made an appointment to meet Slap O'Reilly, his old sidekick. Now you ask me about the politics of harm."

59

"Who's blackmailing him is what he wants me to find out. I can't say anything more, Kyle, and I'd be grateful if you didn't tell anyone else about it."

Broadhead sat at his desk and ran a straightened paper clip through the stem of his charred pipe. "Do me three favors. Steer clear of the law and don't drag me into it."

"That's two favors."

"The third is unrelated. You're planning a surprise bachelor party for me. Don't."

"Who said I'm doing anything of the kind?"

"I've lived in L.A. almost as long as the Dodgers. Some of my spies are in their third generation. I don't want balloons made out of condoms, a stag film with guys who don't take off their socks, a card enrolling me in the Viagra of the Month Club, or any of the myriad other humiliations bridegrooms-to-be are subjected to. Just show up at the wedding with the ring."

Valentino was due at the Motion Picture Country Home in an hour. He got into his car and called Fanta, Broadhead's fiancée.

"Change of plans," he said, when she answered. "The bachelor party's off."

"Says who?"

"Says Kyle."

"Oh, him. Don't pay attention to anything

60

he says. He may think he doesn't want it, but he'll resent it if we don't do something, and he'll blame you as his best man."

"He always means what he says."

"You may have known him longer, but I know him better. Just make sure he doesn't find out again. Don't make any arrangements from the office. Let me know what I can help with. All the bridal stuff's on cruise control at the moment."

"There is something you can do. I'm going to be tied up for a while, and I don't know if there's a cutoff date on refunds. Call the Rexall on Cahuenga and see if you can cancel that order for a case of condoms."

6

Today, Kym Trujillo wore a yellow sundress that showed off her light-caramel complexion to best advantage. She shook his hand from behind her sleek desk and directed him to the flower garden. "Slap's got a green thumb," she said. "His doctor recommended he putter around. Six weeks later we canceled the gardening service."

"Can we speak privately there?"

"The solarium would be best for that."

Sam O'Reilly hadn't changed so much physically Valentino couldn't recognize him from his comic turns in Red Montana movies. The whiskey welts on his long horsey features were more pronounced and when he took off his dilapidated straw hat to wipe the back of a hand across his streaming forehead, his hair was thin, but brushed neatly. Apart from sweat stains the clothes he wore, a red-and-black-checked flannel shirt and overalls, were as tidy as the man himself. He put aside his hoe to shake the archivist's hand, and if anything his grip was stronger than Montana's.

"Kym told me what you do," he said. "It doesn't sound like work for a grown man, but then neither did acting. I don't get many visitors, so I thought it'd help break up another day here in the waiting room."

Valentino noticed the man's grammar was better than that of the characters he'd played on-screen. He was surrounded by a spectacular array of pink, purple, and white bougainvillea, blue hydrangea, blood-red gilia, and at least a dozen other varieties of bloom the visitor couldn't identify. The small patch looked as if a rainbow had unspooled at his feet.

"I'd like to talk to you about Red Montana."

"I was afraid of that."

The actor's sudden scowl reminded him of the need for privacy. He asked him if they could step inside the solarium.

"You mean the greenhouse? The lingo's complicated enough without making up new words all the time when the old ones aren't worn out. I've been around long enough to remember when senior citizens were codgers and meteorologists were weather girls in cute little outfits."

63

He led the way into a steel-framed building paned with huge sheets of glass. The interior was climate-controlled and as bright as a tropical island at midday. Troughs, pots, and flats of budding plants and flowers covered long tables with aisles between. The actor walked without stopping to the opposite end of the building, lifted a small palm out of an earthenware pot, root-ball and all, set it aside, and retrieved something from inside the pot. He offered the flat pint of bourbon to Valentino.

"No, thanks." Montana had told him of his old partner's fondness for alcohol. He had the sinking feeling he'd better get on with the interview while his subject was still able to communicate.

O'Reilly surprised him by unscrewing the cap, placing his nose to the neck of the bottle, inhaling deep, and returning the cap to the bottle and the bottle to its hiding place without taking a drink. He replaced the palm. "I haven't touched a drop in thirty years," he said, "but I'll thank you to keep this a secret. I can do without the booze in my belly, but I'd sure miss the smell."

Valentino had spent the drive over wondering how to approach the subject of his relationship with his former co-star, and had reached his destination without having made a clear decision. But O'Reilly's blunt manner made up his mind for him.

"Montana said you drank your way out of your job at Republic and never forgave him for not putting in a good word for you at the studio."

"He said *that*? Well, that's one thing about him hasn't changed. He lied when he sang 'Jingle Bells.' It's true my thirst cost me my livelihood, but I never blamed anyone for it but me. I never asked anyone to bail me out, and if I ever did, it wouldn't be him I asked. He never gave anybody anything without expecting something back, and I sure wasn't in a position to do him any favors even if I wanted to. I'd rather they fished me out of the tar pits with a belly full of Old Jackhammer."

"Then what happened between you?"

The old cowboy uncorked his famous saddlebag grin and assumed his screen dialect. "Well, son, if it waren't money, and it sure as shootin' waren't politics or religion, what you reckon's left?"

"Sex?"

"We didn't bandy the word about so much in those days," he said, slipping back into everyday grammar. "It covers a lot more ground than it used to; back then it meant only one thing, and that didn't come till you got to know someone a whole lot better. It was the *Wyoming Waltz* shoot, Dixie's second. It was supposed to be a bit part like the first; she was the daughter of the small-time rancher getting squeezed out by the wicked cattle baron, had one line. But in the rushes, the brass could see the camera falling in love with her. They gave her three good scenes, which she stole, right along with my heart. We were on location in Monument Valley, never mind the place was farther away from Wyoming than Burbank. All the wranglers and cowboy extras were showing off for her, doing rope tricks and handstands on their saddles, and I was right there among them.

"She took a shine to me, for some reason, and we spent all our time together between scenes. We were shooting second unit then, no dialogue, nothing for a big star like Red Montana to bother himself with. He didn't show up until three weeks in, and that was the end of it for yours truly. The minute he stepped out of that custom Caddy pimped out like a longhorn steer, he locked his eyes square on Dixie."

O'Reilly tugged on a pair of heavy gardening gloves, signaling the interview was nearing its end.

"Well, that was it for yours truly. How can

66

the comic relief compete with the star of the show? Montana renegotiated his contract and the ink wasn't dry on it before she wrote her name once again on a marriage license next to Montana's."

"You must resent them both."

"Not Dixie. Hollywood's changed, but not when it comes to bulldogging an opportunity when it's standing right in front of you. Looks? Any carhop inside a hundred miles of this spot would pop your eyes clean out of your head, and not one in a hundred got within a mile of a screen test. Talent? Throw a saddle in any direction and you hit a high school where the drama queen can act licks around any leading lady you care to name, and she'll never see the inside of the private elevator to a producer's office. Right place at the right time: sheer dumb luck. You can't blame a girl for striking when the iron's hot, because, brother, it cools off faster than a sizzling skillet in a flash flood.

"Anyway, I don't think she felt anything for me, apart from a good time in pleasant company. I did for her, though. Montana knew that, and he went after her the same way he went after money and glory, and God help whoever got in his way. Resent *him*? Hell, yes; but not for what he did to me. For what he did to Dixie."

"Why Dixie? She's the model of a successful woman."

O'Reilly's lip curled. "This town's got to you same as all the rest: You've got success mixed up with money. My mother was the most successful woman I ever knew, and I knew all the great ladies in the industry from Gloria Swanson to Marilyn, God rest her soul." He crossed himself. "My mother had the love of a good man her whole life, and she raised two sons who loved her. One's dead, the other's on his way, but she went to her grave knowing that. What's Red ever given Dixie? A big barn of a house with no children to fill it up and a stuffed horse."

Valentino knew the secret then of the flourishing flowers in the garden; they throve on the bitter compost of Sam O'Reilly's hatred for his old co-star.

"All this happened almost sixty years ago," he said. "That's a long time to hold a grudge."

"I'm not angry I lost Dixie. I was for a long time, but I got over it. You can get over anything, including a bite from a diamondback that swells your leg big as a calf and gives you a fever hot enough to fry bacon on your forehead. Liquor helps in both cases. If I'd married her I'd have messed that up just like I messed it up with the woman I did marry."

His face went slack then; no trace of the long, humorous features of the perennial foil he'd made his stock-in-trade. He blinked rapidly. "Who'd you say you were with, again? My memory isn't so good these days."

Valentino realized he was losing him, and stepped up the pace.

"The Film Preservation Department at UCLA. I'm trying to track down a movie Dixie Day made before she met Red Montana." He'd cooked up the half-lie on the way to the Home.

"I wouldn't know anything about it. I'd only been going out with her a couple of weeks when Montana showed up. We met at a cast party. She came there with a cameraman. I'll remember his name in a minute." His mind wandered. "I hear Dixie's in a bad way."

"The doctors don't give her long."

"I'm sorry. She was a good old gal, too good for Montana. If that crumb shoves her full of straw and sets her up on display I'll kill him."

"The cameraman," Valentino prompted.

"Cameraman?" When the muscles in O'Reilly's features let go, he truly looked old. "Oh. Dick Hennessey. I remember his name on account of the studio bounced him later. Moonlighting, it was."

"That hardly seems worth firing him."

"It did then. It was a big scandal at the time. Not like now, when any little old lady can march right up to a counter and rent *Deep Throat.* Imagine that; in my day you had to know a guy who knew a guy, and take your chances you weren't doing business with the vice squad."

The film archivist felt his temperature rising. "You mean — ?"

O'Reilly looked piteous. "Smut, son. Cops busted Dixie's date for shooting stag films on the side."

7

"Nice of you to drop in." Ruth, putting on what must have been a third coat of blood-red nail polish, jerked her chin toward a ramshackle stack of messages resting on her desk. Valentino wondered if she ever bothered to remove the previous coats before applying a fresh one.

They were written in her spiky hand on sheets from the cheery pad she used with a beaming sun in one corner. He guessed it had been a gift from someone who didn't know her very well. He turned away from the fumes wafting from her nail brush to clear his eyes and read.

At first he couldn't remember whom Evan and Laura Overholt were; then he recalled the encounter with the psychologist and her attorney husband in the Red Montana and Dixie Day Museum. They'd offered to help him out with his quest for an experienced woodcarver for The Oracle renovation.

He pocketed the messages as non-urgent. "I'll be in my office."

"You want directions?"

"Ruth, do you even know what my job is?"

"Watching movies and gallivanting all over Southern California on the university's ticket. Meanwhile your immediate supervisor locks himself up in his office all day, writing love letters to himself. At least when this building was a power plant it made a contribution."

She seemed about to expand on the subject when the telephone rang on her console. She lifted the receiver awkwardly between her palms. "It's for you. That girl from the morgue." She stuck it at him.

He extricated it. Educating her as to the nature of Harriet Johansen's responsibilities to the forensics division of the Los Angeles Police Department had proved fruitless.

"I heard from our new friends," Harriet said.

"Me, too. They're persistent."

"They're probably like us, starved for another couple to hang out with. Are we free for dinner tonight? They live in one of those houses hanging on by their eyebrows to Laurel Canyon."

"That depends. Is there rain in the forecast?"

"Not all those places are fodder for mud-slides. It could be fun, Val. You remember fun?"

"I have a vague recollection." It dated back to before he'd acquired the most exasperating reclamation project since Shakespeare's Globe.

"I'll put it in terms you'll understand," she said. "Maybe they can help you out with your whittling problem."

"What time?"

"Sevenish. I'm quoting."

"Pick you up at six-thirtiesh."

In his office, shingled all over with posters, lobby cards, and publicity stills curling at the edges, he cleared a stack of cans containing reels awaiting editing and found his computer. After forty-five minutes of browsing, he came across a paragraph reproduced from a copy of *Variety* dated June 10, 1970:

CAMERAMAN FOUND DEAD

Van Nuys, June 9 — The body of Richard Hennessey, 52, a former cameraman with Republic, was found today in his apartment. Police are investigating the death as an apparent suicide, and believe the victim to have been dead at least three days. Hennessey was fired from the studio in 1955 after his conviction on several counts of producing lewd entertainment contributing to the delinquency of minors.

Hoping to uncover details of the vice case, Valentino made the mistake of Googling PORNO — HOLLYWOOD, and spent the next hour expunging disturbing graphics from his screen.

He buzzed Ruth. "Is Dr. Broadhead in his office?"

"Nope." She blew air, ostensibly onto her fourth or fifth coat of varnish. "Out gallivanting."

He sighed. "Where, pray tell?"

"You might want to stop at Beverly Hills Stables on the way and rent a horse."

Through Kyle Broadhead's influence, Valentino had a lifetime pass to Universal's theme amusement park, established on the site of the studio's back lot. When the tram continued past the old western-town set without stopping, the passenger made his way to the seat behind the driver and asked him why.

The man was a Chicano, with a solid bar of moustache that suggested he spent his off-duty hours answering casting calls for Mexican bandidos; his accent, however, was

Midwestern. "Closed for repairs. That last shaker cracked a couple of foundations."

He got off ahead of the Bruce the Shark exhibit from *Jaws* and made his way back on foot, against a tide of tourists living through their camera phones in Chinatown, Jack the Ripper's London, and the Bavarian village where the locals had chased the Frankenstein monster with torches, pitchforks, bloodhounds, and their trainers. He turned a corner in ancient Rome and found himself standing at the main four corners in Anytown-West-of-St.-Louis. Hollywood in general was a wide-awake acid trip, but nowhere was the woozy sensation of traveling through space and time so vivid as in the remaining vestiges of the days before on-location shooting, when the Dream Factory was a self-contained world, spinning independently of the rest of the universe; how fitting that the last studio that hadn't sold off its miles of exterior sets to realtors should be named *Universal.*

Here, he thought, as he followed his long shadow down the dusty main street, was where William S. Hart, Randolph Scott, Broncho Billy Anderson, John Wayne, Joel McCrea, Sunset Carson, Tom Mix, Lash LaRue, Hoot Gibson, Jock Mahoney, Harry Carey, and so many other giants in spurs and Stetsons had galloped aboard lathered horses to outdraw the equally iconic villains in black hats: Zachary Scott, Walter Huston, Barton MacLane, Noah Beery, Sr., Glenn Strange, Bruce Cabot, John Carradine, Lee Marvin, Lee Van Cleef, John Ireland, and at least a dozen other two-legged varmints, all of whom bore a suspicious resemblance to Brian Donlevy. One could almost smell the acrid stench of spent black powder.

No construction was going on, although barricades at the entrances to all the streets warned visitors to keep out, and stacks of fresh lumber and piles of foundation stone and sacks of mortar deposited here and there spoke of repairs to be done. The inevitable frame church at the end of the central street appeared to have sustained the worst damage from the most recent tremor: Plywood took the place of stained glass in the windows and stout planks were nailed securely across the front door to prevent curiosity-seekers from entering and climbing to the compromised stability of the bell tower.

Valentino passed a general store, a bank, and a jail, pausing at each no longer than to recall what scenes had taken place before each; he had a pretty good idea in which building Broadhead would be found.

At length he mounted the boardwalk in front of a false-front structure with a sign mounted above the porch reading DRY GULCH SALOON. He pushed through the bat-wing doors and waited just inside for his eyes to adjust themselves to the dim interior. The first thing he noticed was a stack of signs similar in design to the one outside leaning against a wall, assigning the location of the business to Carson City, Deadwood, Cripple Creek, and the inevitable Purgatory; the place required only the addition to the street outside of soap-flake snow or powdery dust or mud prepared in a cement mixer to bring it into line with the frozen Rockies, the arid desert, or any one of a hundred mining camps in the rain-drenched Pacific Northwest.

The rest of the décor he could have supplied with his eyes closed: the nude reclining on canvas above the beer taps, the long, ornately carved bar, the strategically placed spittoons, the green-baize-covered poker tables, the moth-eaten buffalo head overlooking the doorway marked LADIES' ENTRANCE.

Oh, and the piano; which had stopped playing abruptly the moment Valentino entered. He grinned at that.

"I always wanted that to happen when I

came into a saloon," he said.

"I know." Kyle Broadhead, seated on the turning stool in front of the scarred upright, ran a finger the length of the keyboard, executing an expert glissando. "You've mentioned it often enough."

"I didn't know you could play."

"My mother took in boarders, including a music teacher who used to play in the neighborhood theater until talkies did her out of a job. She gave me lessons in lieu of rent. She was a hundred and fifty years old and smelled like Skoal."

"What was that you were playing?"

" 'Buffalo Gals,' what else? To watch any old horse opera you'd think it was the only number in the repertoire. Actually, those old-time hacks were well up on Vivaldi and the other great masters of Europe; but that's just a little too sophisticated for the Hollywood frontier, where the Pony Express went on forever and everybody dropped his G's except the wicked banker. I'd offer you a drink, but the bottles behind the bar are filled with colored water and the door to the storeroom opens onto a Martian colony."

The professor looked more rumpled than usual, with dust turning his sweaty features to sandpaper and his beloved tweed hat perched on the back of his head. His shoes were stained brown along with the cuffs of his trousers; obviously he'd walked all the way from the park entrance without bothering with the tram. He leaned on one elbow and plunked out the opening bars of *The Marriage of Figaro* with the blunt fingers of his other hand.

Valentino slid a chair propped upside down on a nearby table, righted it, and straddled the seat. "What brings you out here to the middle of nowhere, stranger?"

Broadhead plunked out the opening bars of "My Darling Clementine." "I hit the wall writing about the psychology behind the popularity of westerns and came here for inspiration by osmosis."

"How's that working out?"

"I've developed an almost irresistible impulse to go out and buy the most expensive pair of cowboy boots in Beverly Hills."

"That could be your answer. Maybe it's not so much mental as visceral; some kind of sense-memory unique to Americans."

"I'm English on both sides."

"I'm Scotch-Italian, but I've seen every John Wayne western since *The Big Trail* several times. Almost half the pioneers were born in Europe or Asia."

The professor abandoned Clementine for

something abstract. He didn't seem to be listening to his own music.

"What's the real reason, Kyle? You always change the subject whenever inspiration comes up."

He stopped playing abruptly, sending a frisson up Valentino's spine; *that* sounded like what happened when a bad man entered an old-time saloon.

"You're still planning a bachelor party, aren't you?"

He hesitated. That was the last thing he expected in those surroundings. "You told me not to."

"You forget I've known you since you were in my film class. You always answer with a non sequitur when you want to duck the question. I have this recurring nightmare of letting myself into my house and having all the lights come on and pink confetti showering down like acid rain."

"Just to be clear, I had no plans for confetti."

"We'll hold it here. Use my name when you call the park manager. He owes me; never mind what."

The other looked around. "Well, I guess it doesn't get any more man-friendly than this."

"There's more."

Broadhead rotated a quarter-turn on the stool, drew an envelope from inside his tweed jacket, and held it out.

Valentino looked at it. " 'Cremation Services'?"

"You'll start getting them too, after you turn fifty. Look inside."

He drew out a circular showing a variety of urn designs for ash storage. He turned it over and looked at a list of names written in the professor's looping hand on the back.

"You're invited too, of course," said Broadhead. "These are some people I've known since the Flood. Some of them are probably dead. Good luck finding the others."

"Why the sudden change of heart?"

"Several reasons, chief among them the imminence of my own immolation. I'm about to marry a woman who wasn't born yet when my computer came off the line. She'll likely be the death of me, with any luck. This may be my last chance to see these people."

"This morbid streak is something new. Are you ill?"

"I have it on the authority of my personal physician that I can reasonably expect to accept a call from the President on the occasion of my hundredth birthday. I set up the appointment the day I proposed."

"I thought it was Fanta who did the proposing."

"You know, now that I think back, I'm not sure either of us did. Do you suppose there's a loophole there?"

"You know you don't mean that."

"I was thinking of her, not me."

Valentino looked again at the list. "I haven't the faintest idea where to start."

Broadhead drew a smile across his rubbery face.

"What's it say on your business cards?"

" 'Film Detective,' " Valentino said. "I've wondered all this time how long it would take you to rub my nose in it."

"Now that that's settled, let's talk about why you came looking for me. Starting with what the person you're after has on Red Montana."

8

Outside the saloon, the distinctly non-frontier noise of heavy equipment backing up shattered the illusion of a place out of time.

"You're vacillating in your dotage," Valentino said. "You were just as adamant about not wanting to know what I'm up to as you were against a bachelor party."

"Have you ever known me to dote, even in jest? Medicine isn't an exact science. I may rack up triple digits, or I may expire tomorrow at my desk. There's a reason someone plays the organ and the guest of honor wears black at both weddings and funerals. This crusade may be my last. I'm loath to think a trip down the aisle may be my final adventure."

He turned back toward the piano, hovered his hands above the keyboard, then laid them in his lap and faced Valentino again. "Promise me, if I expire in Fanta's arms, you'll help her dress me and throw me down the stairs. I don't want to go into university legend as a *Playboy* cartoon."

"I'll have to run that past your widow." The archivist rose from his chair and paced the room. "I don't need to tell you none of this leaves this building. Red Montana has engaged me to find out who's shaking him down over an ill-advised film Dixie Day starred in two generations ago. Apparently it still exists."

"Hard or soft-core?"

"What's the difference?"

"The same as the difference between rape and the attempt. It all has to do with whether penetration took place."

He felt his face redden. "I've no idea if it did or didn't. With any luck I never will. Kyle, I wish you'd at least pretend to be shocked. These are icons we're talking about."

"You've lived here long enough to know the sunsets are painted and the stairs don't go anywhere. Considering the recent past, I'm surprised anybody would get his bowels in an uproar over just a stag film. Careers have been built on them."

"I'd agree, if it were anybody but Dixie Day."

"And what has the cowboy king offered

you in the way of compensation?"

"A complete print of *Sixgun Sonata,* his first feature with Dixie. It's a long-lost item."

"Of course it is. Uncovering the non-existent is your stock-in-trade. Is it worth it? You know, those three-day oaters weren't exactly *High Noon.* An airplane might fly low over a stagecoach chase and they never made a second take."

"What I saw looked better than the average. In any case, I'm not a critic. I can't afford to pass up a chance to fill in a break in the DNA chain." He stopped pacing. "There's a risk factor as well. He threatened to destroy the print if I turned him down."

"Of course he did."

"More cynicism?"

"Practical supposition. Montana's CEO of a multinational business, with his own seat on the New York Stock Exchange and a presence on half a dozen boards of directors. You don't get that kind of success doing rope tricks and shooting the gun out of Black Bart's hand. A man with more than six zeroes in his checking account might as well wear a patch over one eye and drop an *'arrr!'* into every conversation."

"So now you're a socialist?"

"I didn't say I disapproved. Abe Lincoln

pushed for the transcontinental railroad because he used to represent the Union Pacific and owed it his presidency. Great men are almost never good men. What have you dug up so far?"

"Not much. Slap O'Reilly told me Dick Hennessey shot the porno picture. He was a house director at Republic until the studio fired him for moonlighting in the blue trade. Unfortunately, he committed suicide more than forty years ago."

"I seem to recall the name," Broadhead said.

"I'm not surprised. You probably know all the aliases Rin Tin Tin used when he checked into a hotel with Lassie."

"Lassie was a female impersonator. The Kaiser would never have allowed Rin Tin Tin into the German Army if he were gay. I'm thinking more recent. I need my computer."

"Abracadabra." Valentino took out his smartphone. "Birthday gift from Harriet," he said. "Are you still using the same password?"

"I don't believe in changing it. Sooner or later you're bound to come up with one easy to crack."

Outside, the truck or whatever it was had stopped backing up. Something made a hideous wrenching noise that reminded the archivist of a Godzilla movie, followed by a clatter — a spill of bricks, perhaps — and a gonging sound; that would be the bell being removed from the church tower while it was under repair.

Broadhead had come to the same conclusion. "It's always the place of worship that gets hit, have you noticed? You'd think atheists would make more of that than they do."

Valentino entered ROKUZ. The professor's computer file opened like an enormous blossom, displaying his screensaver, a vintage photo of the old headquarters of Famous-Players Lasky (later Paramount), founded by Adolph Zukor, whose name spelled backwards no hacker had since stumbled upon. He handed the phone to the professor, who slid a pair of heavy black-rimmed glasses onto his nose and promptly bewildered the Internet by mashing three keys with his thumb. Without saying a word, his friend reached over and applied his index finger to the chore.

"Richard Hennessey, Jr.," Broadhead said after a moment. "Candy Box Pictures. The coconuts don't fall far from the plastic palm trees in this town."

9

The address listed for Candy Box Pictures was in Pasadena. Valentino was calculating whether to drive out there that day or wait till morning when his phone rang. He didn't recognize the number, so he let voice mail take a message.

"Hi, this is Laura Overholt," said the chipper voice on the recording. "Just calling to tell you not to bring anything tonight. Just yourselves."

He'd already forgotten he and Harriet had agreed to dine with their new friends. Just as he finished listening the phone rang again. It was Harriet.

"Where are you?" she asked. "I called your office, but Ruth said you were off playing cowboys and Indians. Is it time to start worrying about her?"

"I stopped worrying about Ruth the day I met her. She asked me what happened to her chicken salad sandwich. I was working there a month before she stopped mistaking me for a delivery boy." He told her where he was and that he was with Kyle.

"That's even harder to picture," she said. "Who's that playing the piano?"

Broadhead was plunking out a lively rendition of "Camptown Races." Valentino said, "You wouldn't believe me if I told you. What's going on?"

She relayed Laura Overholt's message. He said he already had it.

"They're beyond persistent now," he added. "Can you say 'pushy'?"

"Don't be such a wet blanket. Don't you remember what it was like not to have anyone you could hang out with?"

"Are you saying you're tired of hanging out with plain old me?"

"Not when you're being so charming."

She was right. He should be grateful to Evan for offering the services of his wood-carving client. "I'm sorry. It's been a day."

"That's better. Do you want me to call and cancel?"

He looked at his watch. It was almost five.

"I wouldn't ask you to do that on such short notice. I'll see you in an hour and a half." They said good-bye. "There goes Pasadena," he told Kyle.

"If only that were true."

"Do you need a lift?"

"No, I rented a crossover. My neighbor thinks anyone who doesn't drive a gas-hog is a card-carrying Communist. I'm going to park it overnight in front of his house."

"I'll let you know how I make out with that list."

"Just don't tell me which names belong to corpses. It's depressing enough just picking out a wedding cake."

The house was a Frank Lloyd Wright, or close enough to pass. It reminded Valentino of James Mason's lair near Mt. Rushmore in *North by Northwest:* two different levels of rectangular construction resembling a deck of playing cards in mid-cut.

Evan Overholt opened the door. He wore a bright orange sweater vest over a shirt with the cuffs turned back, pleated slacks, and Italian loafers with tassels. Clear liquid showed in a glass slightly smaller than a fire bucket in his right hand. "Right on time," he greeted, tilting his head toward a novelty clock mounted on a wall of the foyer. The small hand pointed to "sevenish."

One of *those* couples, Valentino thought.

"Where's little Jack?" Harriet peered beyond their host's shoulder.

"With his grandparents. He gets a little

hyper around guests. If I'd been half so out-going at his age, I'd be a Supreme Court justice by now."

A man he'd never met stood in the center of a sunken living room. He was about Valentino's age and had on a denim shirt with the tail out over faded jeans, well-broken-in sneakers on his feet. Next to him was Laura Overholt, who came forward to shake the visitors' hands. She was slim-hipped in black Capri pants, a short-sleeved silk blouse, and sandals.

"Thanks so much for coming," she said. "I told Evan it was rude to invite anyone so late. He was supposed to call you this morn-ing."

"I can cite fifty years of legal precedents word-for-word, but remembering a simple errand is always a challenge," said her husband. "Mr. Valentino, Miss Johansen, this is Victor Stavros, Junior."

"The client," said Harriet, pushing her small hand into his large one. "How's the case coming along?"

"Evan says we'll wear out the State De-partment eventually." The guest had a deep voice and dark curly hair that made him look younger than he was; Valentino amended his earlier assumption, adding ten years to his age. "I'm sorry Pop isn't here to

91

meet you. We didn't know until you accepted the invitation that he was planning to visit his club."

"It's a glorified bar," said Evan. "A Greco-American hangout. Victor Senior goes there to drink retsina, play cards, and speak nothing but Greek all night."

"Ironic, isn't it?" Victor Junior looked pained. "I'm fighting to stay in this country, and Dad wants to go back home, but we can't afford the fare until this mess is over. He's wanted it ever since my mother passed."

Valentino said, "I look forward to meeting him. He sounds like just the artisan I need for the Oracle."

"Don't use the word 'artisan' around Pop. He's proud to call himself a woodcarver, like his father and grandfather. He's never really gotten over being disappointed that I'm all thumbs with anything but a drawing pencil."

"Junior inherited the old man's modesty," said Laura. "He's one of the best architects in the state."

The living room was comfortably furnished in blue leather with an onyx fireplace and a Degas poster mounted above the mantel. Evan was fixing drinks from a butler's cart when his wife announced that

92

dinner would be delayed.

"Our cook's on vacation," she said. "I'm a fair hand with salmon, but I was so busy telling Evan not to forget to call you I forgot to take it out of the freezer until this afternoon." She turned to Victor Stavros, Junior. "Why don't you take our guests to the Ilium and introduce them? Everything should be ready in half an hour."

Stavros sprang from his seat. "It's just down the hill. Pop loves his work almost as much as Greece. If you hit it off, maybe he'll stop talking about home for a while."

Valentino hesitated. "I'd hate to desert our hosts."

Evan said, "You'll be doing us a favor. If I lend a hand in the kitchen, we'll be eating in half the time, and anyway the noise in that place is murder on my delicate ears. Eight o'clock, Victor?"

"If the old man doesn't lure me into a wrestling match." Stavros the Younger cracked his knuckles in anticipation.

"How is it I didn't know this place existed?"

Valentino had to shout to be heard above the din. The air in the cramped barroom was larded with the din of voices raised in laughter and dispute and a riot of strings pouring from an old-fashioned jukebox. The heat of a capacity crowd, each member putting out 98.6 degrees, was tropical, the smell of sweat containing a texture all its own.

"Probably because last month it was a Laundromat," Harriet shouted back. "You're forgetting where we live."

The walls, craquelured like those of an ancient ruin, were decorated with prints made from paintings of heroes and gods out of Greek literature, interspersed with sepia photographs of the Acropolis, fishing boats moored near the shore of the Aegean, Mt. Olympus wearing its perennial crown of snow, and burly wrestlers in tights and bare glistening chests. The shelves behind the bar bristled with bottles of retsina, ouzo, and other exotic Mediterranean spirits in bottles with Greek labels. What appeared to be a mature olive tree grew in a wooden bucket in one corner. The bartender shaved his head and curled his handlebars after the fashion of the wrestlers in the ancient photos: Valentino had the impression he might be asked to show him his passport before he'd serve him. Hollywood, however, was never far removed from any establishment in the area: On a huge flat-panel TV screen, Steve Reeves as Hercules burst free of iron shackles on a continuous loop with the sound turned off. The clientele was almost exclusively male, made up mostly of old men with white paintbrush beards in berets and striped jerseys.

"Pop's never hard to find," said Victor Junior, inclining his curly head toward a group gathered on foot around a table next to a disintegrating brown poster evidently advertising for volunteers to serve in the Balkan War.

They approached the table, where members of the crowd parted reluctantly to afford them a glimpse of the occupants. One, a wiry man in his seventies with gold-rimmed glasses perched atop his thatch of blinding white hair, sat locked in combat with another man of the same vintage, albeit built along the lines of an ox in a white shirt with collar spread to expose a thatch of black chest hair mixed with splinters of gray and a five o'clock shadow as black as many men's full beards. A tortured grin, as white as his opponent's hair, was nailed in the center of this growth, eyes fixed on the man seated across from him rather than their hands clenched together, elbows planted on the table. A jumble of Euro bills with a Minotaur engraved on each quivered on the surface from the sheer effort of the combatants.

Victor Junior said something in Greek to

the nearest spectator, who answered in the same tongue.

"It won't be long now," reported the first. "They've been at it forty-five minutes."

"Which one's your father?" Harriet asked.

"The one on the left; the one who gave me my good looks."

The grinning man with the black stubble looked like an older, more well-fed version of their new acquaintance.

Valentino asked how big the bet was.

"It doesn't matter, as you'll see in a moment."

With a sudden crash, Victor Senior slammed the white-haired man's hand to the table, dislodging some of the currency onto the floor, where it was immediately scooped up by a member of the audience. The winner roared, snatched up the rest of the cash, and threw it into the air. Very few of the bills made it to the floor before they were claimed by the watchers.

Junior shook his head. "Happens every time, and it's usually Pop. I shudder to think how far what he's thrown away would go toward winning my case; but he's a great believer in mutual independence."

From a hip pocket, Senior retrieved more money and shouted something to the bartender, who came over to claim it, placed a foaming mug in front of the customer, and set up drinks for the crowd already waiting at the bar. The loser stood, bowed at his conqueror with exaggerated dignity, and elbowed his way up to the foot rail, where a shot glass awaited him with a clear liquid inside it that was probably as lethal as it looked harmless.

Senior recognized his son, and got up to slap his back with such force Valentino felt it in his.

"Congratulations," said the son. "How many does this make in a row?"

"You count. I'm too thirsty." The older man lifted his mug and drank off half the contents, finishing with a Homeric belch.

"Pop, this is the man I told you about and his friend."

A transformation accompanied Harriet's introduction. Victor Stavros Senior rose, smoothed back his thick head of hair, wiped his palm on his trousers, and took her hand as if it were made of crystal, bowing over it. "It is American women I will miss," said he. "Even if they are too skinny."

She flushed to her collar. "American women will miss you if you continue to talk like that."

The film archivist, whose hand was not made of crystal, behaved as if it was, burying it deep in the big man's fist to protect his fingers. Even so he felt the grip as far as his elbow.

"Indian or Brazilian?"

Flustered, Valentino said, "I'm American, sir."

"I speak of the mahogany. Indian carves easier, but Brazilian holds its shape better. Brazilian is better. I am not lazy, and I wish my work to last."

He realized then they were discussing terms. "My designer says Central American. There's some trouble with importing it from the Brazilian rainforest."

"Fa! If the bastards have their way everything will be cherry. I am sorry for my crude language," he told Harriet. "This is no place for a young lady."

"I think the coffee house is closed," said his son.

"What I spent here, they can open it up."

After a moment's conversation with the bartender, that individual produced a key ring the size of a coconut and unlocked a door behind the bar with a sign on it reading AUTHORIZED PERSONNEL ONLY, with presumably the same sentiment repeated beneath it in Greek. He leaned through the opening, turned on a light, and returned to his duties at the bar. Senior led his party

98

into a room the same size as the one they'd left, but which seemed larger for the lack of clutter and crowd. The walls were white-washed, there were a dozen or so tables with chairs upended atop them, and the atmosphere smelled deliciously of rich, coarse-ground coffee beans. Here the ambience was less testosterone-fueled: A beautifully rendered mural of a Mediterranean seaport at sunset covered most of one wall and tasteful miniature sculptures of ancient goddesses were dotted about.

The Stavroses righted four chairs and they all sat down at a round table. Valentino had come prepared with photos of the interior of The Retro, some archival taken at the peak of its splendor, others showing the work currently in progress. Senior hooked on a pair of readers to examine close-ups of the woodwork in the vintage pictures.

"This is all hand-carved," he said. "You can see the marks of the tools." He shuffled to one of the later shots. "Much is missing, and what is there has fed the termites since before I was born. Barbarians have blurred the details with many coats of cheap paint, probably lead-based. It would take me five years to replace it all."

"Doing handwork," Valentino said hopefully.

"Yes."

"I can't wait five years. Could you do it with lathes and like that?"

"Lathes, shapers, and moulders would allow me to complete it in six months." The old man shook his head. "It would be a shame not to do it as it was originally done. More than a shame. A sin."

Valentino said, "Let's be sinners."

10

When it came time for an estimate, Valentino was stung by the amount, but relieved it wasn't worse; he'd feared the old cabinetmaker would want to charter a flight back to the Old Country on that one job. They sealed the deal over drinks retrieved from the bar by Victor Junior. Senior finished a tall glass of ouzo in one draught. The film archivist sipped at his, found it almost sickeningly sweet, like peppermint schnapps, and almost certainly lethal to the senses in doses not much larger. Junior abstained. Astonishingly, Harriet emptied her glass in a few minutes.

"What?" She met Valentino's stare. "A woman in a predominately male job has to learn to hold her own."

"I've never seen you drink anything stronger than a glass of white wine."

"You think I drink in front of you the same way I drink in front of cops? Especially

Sergeant Cosmatos."

Feeling challenged, he took a longer drink. The stuff settled into the pit of his stomach as heavily as sediment.

Senior, approving, called for another round; but his son, perhaps taking into account his fellow guests, looked at his watch and said the Overholts were expecting them. The old man scraped back his chair and stood all in one volcanic movement. Rising, Valentino felt a balloon inflate inside his head and steadied himself against the table. Harriet, the iron woman, was already on her feet, steady as something carved from cool marble.

Junior cupped the film archivist's elbow discreetly with one hand, helping him restore his balance. "You've just sampled the secret behind how Athens whipped Sparta. One whiff of the stuff puts me out for the count."

"Here's a tip," Harriet whispered. "Don't drink water on an empty stomach for twelve hours. The chemical reaction's murder."

The dinner was quite pleasant. Valentino managed to forget his exhausting day over a plate of tasty salmon, flaky and perfectly cooked with a tangy horseradish sauce, new potatoes, garden-fresh peas from the local farmers' market, and a delicious tiramisu for dessert, which Laura confessed was bought from a bakery. Evan uncorked a Napa Valley Chardonnay to go with the entrée; this the film archivist declined, still recovering as he was from his first taste of Greek nitroglycerine. Victor Senior drank three glasses, and showed no signs of inebriation when they retired to the living room with coffee, where he serenaded the assembly in his deep baritone, singing a country ballad in his native tongue while accompanying himself on the lute. His audience, without understanding the lyrics, was moved by the throbbing emotion in his voice.

Smiling somewhat shyly at the applause, the old man thumbed a tear from each eye and patted the belly of the lute. "I cannot carry a tune without this. It belonged to my grandfather, who fought the Turks under Kemal Pasha in 1922; his spirit is trapped inside and only emerges when it is played. I was strumming it on the ship to America when a gust of wind tore it out of my hands and swept it overboard. The captain refused to drop anchor to rescue a musical instrument, so I dove in after it."

"Fortunately, the captain wasn't a Turk," Junior added.

They discussed psychology (Laura's contribution), the law (Evan's), criminal forensics (Harriet's), and architecture (Junior's), which led to the ongoing rescue of The Oracle from rubble and then movies. Valentino, fully alert now, would have gone on more about old-time Hollywood trivia had not Harriet, somewhat ostentatiously, dragged out her cell and said, "Gosh, it's almost eleven. I have a brain to weigh first thing in the morning."

Evan glanced at the clock on the mantel — black, glossy, and featureless but for a pair of illuminated hands. "I suppose we should rescue Mom and Dad. Jack knows all their weaknesses when it comes to putting him to bed."

At the door, the hosts and Victor Junior shook their hands warmly, the Overholts vowing, with a ring of sincerity, to repeat the evening. Senior — not, it seemed, as impervious to drink as he appeared — took Valentino in a bear hug the film archivist still felt in his ribs the next morning. Harriet managed to stave off a similar assault by stepping outside as her escort was extricating himself. Senior's scent was a pungent mixture of spirits and sweat that contained its own gravity.

Driving away, Valentino expelled a lungful

of air. "Thanks for breaking us loose. I'm pooped."

"You're starting to sound as ancient as Kyle," Harriet said. "I bet Evan's two years older than you are."

"I guess raising a small boy builds up your stamina. Also he didn't just go a round with Zorba the Greek."

"Maybe if we spend enough time with Laura and Evan, you'll draw off some of that energy for yourself. You'll need it unless you intend to avoid Victor Senior for the next six months."

"You really like them, don't you?"

"Don't you?"

"They seem nice enough, and they're anything but boring. I've never had a better meal or a more enjoyable evening that didn't involve a film."

"High praise. But — ?" The whites of her eyes reflected the light from a passing street-lamp. He sensed challenge.

"It's nothing I can put my finger on. I just feel the same way I did just after I bought the theater and it dawned on me just how much I'd bit off."

"I don't get your meaning."

They left the canyon and turned toward the city. The moon looked harvest yellow behind a scrim of smog. "I'm not sure myself, only that what looked at first like a bargain might wind up costing me a lot more than I can handle."

11

In the morning, Valentino ruled out stopping by the office. He had errands to run, and Ruth would just say something snide about the brevity of the layover. He had a dull headache — the legacy of last night's brush with Hellenistic society — that would have made him a poor sparring partner.

Mercifully, the construction crew that had camped out in The Oracle since the dawn of time was on one of its mysterious sabbaticals, so the pounding in his skull didn't have to compete with the whine of saws and thump of pneumatic hammers. In the once-and-future projection booth where he kept his apartment, he retrieved a bottle of water from the little refrigerator, but after one sip the room stood suddenly on end. He hadn't really believed Harriet's warning about the chemical reaction with ouzo until that moment.

He recapped and put away the bottle,

poured himself a glass of orange juice, and carried it downstairs for his daily inspection — a routine he'd established the day after vandals entered the building when a departing workman had neglected to lock up, and spray-painted imaginative but unprintable graffiti on the freshly plastered walls of the auditorium.

In that room, demolition dust stirred and drifted when he opened the hidden door at the bottom of the steps to the booth. After countless months of chaos, the proposed flagship of the late Max Fink's theatrical fleet had begun to approach something promising someday to start to resemble a movie house. The students Valentino had borrowed from the dean's list in the UCLA art department had restored nearly half the frescoes in the coffers of the ceiling, and cylinders of industrial-strength crimson carpet lay at the ends of the aisles waiting to be unfurled. Square above his head, a hole gave him an unobstructed view of the attic; the chandelier that had filled the hole was in the basement, swathed in bubble wrap to protect its replaced crystal pendants until the time came to rehang it. The screen inside the proscenium arch, made of a new synthetic material advertised as superior to nylon, was rolled securely in the flies; he'd offered The Oracle as the test case for the experimental fabric in return for a steep discount.

Seats had been removed from the orchestra pit to lay out the ornate paneling belonging to the massive pipe organ, whose entrails had been crated and shipped out of town for restoration. This was the most costly single project in the entire renovation process, as the firm was one of only four in the country and had no need to charge competitive rates.

Along one wall lay the remains of the original mahogany fretwork, riddled with termite holes. The exterminator had charged as much just to preserve the remnants for duplication as if he'd bagged the building for spraying; which had led to an inspection by OSHA to make sure construction employees were safe from contamination and several weeks' delay, with the employees still on salary. "A man might raise Atlantis on less," had been Kyle Broadhead's helpful contribution.

He pushed through semitransparent plastic sheeting to enter the foyer. The fifteen-foot-tall double doors had been removed from their hinges and propped against the wall. Their bronze paint was peeling away in pieces precisely the size of fifty-dollar bills.

In the foyer, more plywood had been laid to protect the faux-marble tiles from hobnails. Long narrow boxes and sheets of foam-core board contained the raw material for candy counters. An old-fashioned popcorn wagon slumbered in one corner under a blue plastic tarp.

The statues of Pegasus standing sentry alongside the sweeping staircase (the steps as yet just bare plywood awaiting veneer and carpeting) had been stripped, repainted, and rewired so their eyes glowed red when Valentino manipulated the hidden switch; the first time he'd tried, a shower of electrical sparks had stung his hand and the electrician had snatched up a fire extinguisher to put out a flaming mane.

Of the four restrooms, two were nearly finished, lacking only a water supply to make their gold-painted sinks and sanitary facilities functional; democratically, one was the gentlemen's, one the ladies'. The other two contained piles of razed debris and pasty gray drywall with yet more holes punched in it to make way for a shipment of plumbing currently stalled in a warehouse in Cedar Rapids, Iowa; that situation pended an agreement with management and the International Brotherhood of Teamsters, who apparently wanted to add a state-of-the-art stereo system to their Freightliners.

Valentino had wasted too much time in the past regretting his ineptitude in matters of math; these days he was grateful for it, because it prevented him from adding up just how much of his eventual retirement he'd spent on the old pile since he'd purchased it in a moment of weakness. He just hadn't been able to bring himself to pass it up lest some greedy developer tear down one of L.A.'s few remaining historical treasures to throw up yet another Starbuck's or — even more likely — a parking lot. The film archivist envisioned, in the not-too-distant future, a city built entirely of black asphalt and yellow lines, with German luxury cars parked door-to-door from Cherry Valley to the foothills, interrupted only by a labyrinth of freeways for them to roam aimlessly.

Well, he rationalized, the most impetuous move of his relatively young life had led to one important benefit: Had he not bought the place, with its hidden bonanza of a complete print of Erich von Stroheim's *Greed* — considered lost for most of a century — and the somewhat less pleasant presence of a skeleton belonging to a fifty-year-old homicide, he and Harriet Johansen would never have known each other existed. She alone was worth the prospect of a life of debt beyond this pale. As much as they struck sparks off each other, theirs was the kind of romance usually found only in the cinema. He'd fallen in love with that ideal at age eight in the concrete bunker of the neighborhood picture house in Fox Forage, Indiana.

Valentino wondered, perversely, if The Rialto still stood, and whether it was for sale.

He stepped outside long enough to confirm that the ticket booth was still there, as yet still lacking glass, and to stare up at the gaunt steel framework of the marquee tower, its tangle of wires capped off in preparation for connecting to the neon tubes and electric bulbs that would eventually spell out the name of the enterprise in letters big and bright enough to be read for blocks.

"I seem to recall seeing something like this in the *Hindenburg* newsreels."

He turned, spilling his orange juice, at the sound of the unexpected voice. Kyle Broadhead stood on the sidewalk with his hands in his pockets, dressed in the Ellis Island outfit he always wore on the street; possibly the only tweed suit and cap in Southern California outside the studio wardrobe de-

112

partments.

Valentino brushed his hand at the stain on his T-shirt. "What brings you here this time of day? Ruth must think she missed an earthquake prediction."

"I stopped by the West Hollywood branch of the Los Angeles Public Library to look up Francis X. Bushman's middle name. This wreck is on the way back."

"You know you can look up that kind of thing online."

"The last time I did that, I found out Bigfoot had been seen sharing a strawberry shake with Elvis in the Brown Derby. Anyway, the library is an institution in need of defib. Aren't you curious to know what the X stood for?"

"X."

The professor's face crumpled further than usual with pain. "I don't know why I didn't just call you."

"Probably because coming by was an excuse to see the expression on my face when you asked if I'd lined up any guests for your stag party."

"To which the answer would be no. You were too busy last night dancing with an Athenian in exile. Harriet called the office asking for you," he explained. "She said you left your wallet at her place last night. Not that there'd be anything in it since Day One of this calamity."

Valentino took his phone from his hip pocket and turned it on. She'd tried him twice.

"Speaking of the expression on your face," Broadhead said, "that's the reason I don't own one of the infernal things. People who would commit murder without blinking become racked with guilt when they realize they failed to answer their cells."

"She knows I'm absentminded." He put it away. "I'll get to that list you gave me this afternoon. Right now I was about to see if I can arrange an appointment with the son of Dick Hennessey the pornographer."

Broadhead finished stuffing his blackened blob of pipe and set fire to it. Gales of smoke drifted Valentino's way with its overpowering stench. Ordering his special blend of tobacco from Zagreb was the professor's single extravagance. It had been the only diversion his captors had allowed him when he was imprisoned as a spy in Yugoslavia; a story whose details he had yet to share with his protégé.

"Don't call him that to the son's face. If he knows about it and he's legit, chances are he's blanked out that branch of the family tree, like Joe Kennedy's experiment with bootlegging during Prohibition. Can you give me a lift to the office on the way?"

"Don't tell me you walked all the way from campus."

"Why not? It's a beautiful day. I actually saw a patch of clear sky hovering over Cahuenga. However, it's closing now, and my feet feel like I'm standing on a hot griddle."

After dropping off his mentor, Valentino called the number Broadhead had found for Candy Box Pictures in Pasadena. Richard Hennessey, Jr. answered his own telephone.

"My father was a cameraman," he confirmed. "He passed away a long time ago."

"I'm sorry." The film archivist was sincere, knowing the circumstances of the elder Hennessey's death. "I'm looking for a film he might have shot back in the fifties."

"For Republic?"

"No, it was something on the side."

"Oh, you mean the porno stuff."

Valentino exited the freeway, pulling into a Park 'N' Ride lot. The matter-of-factness of the response required his full concentration. "You knew about that?"

"It wasn't as if he was alone. Back then, if you weren't Robert Alton or James Wong Howe, the crème-de-la-crème behind the lens, the studio paid you a straight contract

115

salary, whether you were shooting *Samson and Delilah* or Francis the Talking Mule. Dad had four mouths to feed; weigh that against the risk of being blacklisted if you were found out. I wouldn't want to live on the difference."

"He told you about it?"

"It was public record. You know he was convicted for contributing to the delinquency of minors."

"I'm afraid I do."

"It was hogwash. He had no control over who saw his stuff, toddlers or dirty old men. He paid a fine, and never worked in the industry again; took what he'd saved and opened his own photo supply shop in Van Nuys. Things changed fast after that. The stuff that sold underground in his day, from the back rooms of barbershops and commercial garages, was tame compared to what any little old lady can rent from the corner video store. It didn't change my feelings toward Dad. I hope I've been half the parent he was to my own kids; for as long as I had him." Sadness crept into his voice for the first time. Valentino let a moment pass before asking his next question.

"Did he say anything about the films themselves?"

"No. Why get anyone else in trouble? The

judge seized every foot he shot and had it burned."

"Is there any chance some of it was missed?"

"Well, nothing's impossible. I'm in the business myself, and if it had a motto, that'd be it. There'd be no market for the stuff, though. The A studios shoot steamier stuff all the time and get away with an R rating."

Valentino let a heavily loaded tractor-trailer rig thunder past while he digested that. "You talk as if you *saw* some of his films."

"Better than that. You're talking to the only former ten-year-old apprentice cinematographer in the industry."

12

Candy Box Pictures worked out of a Queen Anne house on San Diego Boulevard, one of the few local survivors of Gilded Age architecture, dripping with fretwork and lozenge-shaped shingles on all the gables. The film archivist pulled into a small paved parking lot next to a van with a logo of an open heart-shaped box spilling out coils of glossy celluloid, read a sign next to the front door with a picture of Bela Lugosi in full Dracula rig and the legend ENTER FREELY—AND OF YOUR OWN WILL, and walked down a narrow, poorly lit hallway plastered on either side with posters in cheap frames advertising features he'd never heard of: *White House Warlock, Psycho Night Nurses in Chains, Tunnel Rats, Acapulco for Tourists, Supermom vs. the Gopher King, The Phantom of the Frat House,* and a series that looked like cautionary tales for high school driver's ed students, complete with gallons of cadmium red spilled on two-lane blacktops. The output was eclectic to say the least.

Emerging from that gallery into a cavernous room partially illuminated by skylights, he tiptoed among the cables and equipment and empty Coke cans until he found a technician in green coveralls wearing a reversed baseball cap, apparently with nothing to do. The man pointed out a thickset man in shirtsleeves standing in a Klieg-lit oval with a bearded youth in a Santana T-shirt with tattoos to his elbows, possibly a director. In the center of the oval, a couple sat up in bed, the woman smoking, the man with chin raised while a woman wearing a man's shirt with the tails out applied powder to his neck. The couple was plainly naked under the sheet.

Richard Hennessey, Jr., was a ruddy-faced seventy or so, fit-looking despite his girth, with gold chains wound around his neck and his hair dyed glistening black, a fashion faux pas that brought out every line and sag in his tanning-bed-orange face. He shook the visitor's hand with another of those knuckle-busting grips indigenous to everyone connected with Southern California's chief export.

"The exploitation stuff — zombies and slashers — barely pays the rent," he said in the deep, burring voice from the telephone. "The public-service bunkum pays diddly, but I get to plaster my office with certificates from the NEA and the California Highway Patrol. We're shooting a two-reeler for the Playboy Channel; that's where the cash is. Dad'd blush to see it, but I'm told it's big among the shuffleboard crowd here in Pasadena."

"I think our visitor disapproves." The director — he could be nothing else — stroked his beard.

Valentino smiled painfully. "I liked it better when the camera cut away to horses stomping in the stable. It isn't like Hollywood introduced anything new to the process of procreation."

"Predictability's the essence of success," said Hennessey. "No one really likes surprises. Have you eaten?"

It occurred to the visitor that he hadn't.

"Back off a little on the lights," the proprietor told the tattooed youth. "Yesterday's dailies looked like *Albinos in Love*."

"Wait for the editor. Those were flash cuts. I want to disorient the viewers."

"They don't pay the premium to be disoriented. When they look at a breast or a penis they want to know that's what they're looking at. You'll get your chance to be Orson

Welles when Sony calls."

Hennessey and Valentino left the director fingering his chin-whiskers and adjourned to a break room encircled by gleaming counters with a refrigerator and microwave oven built in. Hennessey nuked a pair of prepackaged burritos, poured them each a slug of strong black coffee, and sat down opposite his guest at a Formica-topped table. He picked up his steaming burrito. "All the delights of old Mexico, with all the flavor of uncured drywall. Every penny we take in goes into what you see on-screen."

"I've lived in L.A. most of my life. You don't have to apologize for the food." Valentino bit off a corner and spent the next three minutes chewing shredded gristle steeped in ketchup.

"They're almost bearable when you dunk 'em." Hennessey demonstrated, dipping a corner of his in his mug.

"That's just about the most disgusting thing I've ever seen."

"Don't knock it till you've tried it."

He did. Now his snack tasted like stale coffee and his coffee tasted like uncured drywall.

"Valentino," Hennessey said. "Any relation?"

"If you mean Rudolph, his name wasn't

even Valentino. As to the fashion designer, my father says no. Let's talk about yours."

"Gladly. I owe everything to Dad. He set up a trust fund that helped me get set up in business and stay afloat through several recessions."

"I thought he might have been strapped."

"You mean because he killed himself? He made that decision before he could burn through what he'd saved all his working life."

"I wasn't going to bring up how he died; but was it because of the stigma?"

"Absolutely not. What was the harm? He paid his cast the industry minimum. He didn't put a gun to their heads and he didn't kidnap his audiences and lock them in their living rooms with the projector. No, he lived to work and he loved it. He didn't need the money he made from the stuff he shot on the side; it kept him occupied when he wasn't working for the studios. When they took that away from him, there was no use going on.

"Anyway," he said, rotating his mug between his palms, "that's the face I put on what he did. It took me years to realize I felt the same way. Dad's tragedy was he was ahead of his time. If he'd stuck it out just a couple more years, until *Deep Throat* and

The Devil in Miss Jones . . ." He shrugged, drank. "But maybe not. He worked in film. That grainy stuff they shot on tape would've turned his stomach, and as for digital; well, he edited his own independent stuff, using scissors and splicing tape. Clicking a DE-LETE key's secretarial work."

"You don't think it was irresponsible of him to expose his son to his stag operation at such an early age?"

"I was a Hollywood brat. Back then, the town paved over every depravity you could think of with a thin coating of morality. Even married couples on-screen slept in separate beds. *Off*screen — well, if you want to hear about exposing, talk to the producer who flashed his junk in front of Shirley Temple in his office at Fox. At least my old man taught me a trade."

"Did that trade include anyone famous?"

His host chewed, swallowed. The burrito seemed to require all his concentration. "Your eyes would pop out of your head if I told you the names of the future movie queens who took off their clothes for my father. I could make a fortune off cable if I were that type, and if those films still existed."

"One of them still does."

Valentino watched Hennessey closely, but

123

he showed no reaction, popping the last morsel into his mouth and washing it down with coffee from a mug with a Jayne Mansfield look-alike on the outside whose halter top vanished as the contents were consumed.

"The cops missed some when they raided the studio," he said. "They were being developed in a custom lab at the time. I remember Dad saying something about it, but I don't know who was in any of them."

"You never screened them?"

"I was afraid if I did and I recognized someone, I'd be tempted to do something about it. The old man would've haunted me if I did. He was a pornographer, not a shakedown artist."

Valentino started to ask something else, but a sharp movement of the mug in Hennessey's hand silenced him. The young actor from the soundstage had entered the room, wearing nothing but a towel around his waist. He nodded at the occupants, poured a cup of steaming water from a large stainless steel container, dandled a tea bag inside, and padded on out dipping it up and down.

"Can't be too careful," the producer said when the door drifted shut behind the man. "The tabloids in this town survive on the tidbits they buy from small-time actors." He sipped from his mug, his eyes on his visitor's. "What's this about, anyway?"

He decided not to mention blackmail after all, lest he lose cooperation. There was just enough truth in what he said instead to put it across.

"I'm negotiating over a certain actress's earliest-billed performance. If it turns out it *wasn't* her film debut, the value takes a dive along with UCLA's credibility. I have to confirm or deny the stag footage still exists."

"That sounds like lose-lose. If you find it, you can prove the former, but you can't prove the latter, short of combing through every frame ever shot in this town. If it's the former, you've got a hot potato that can only devalue the whole project. Ever hear of a model named Helga?"

Valentino shook his head.

"She posed for a series of nudes for Norman Rockwell, but when the paintings came up for auction after his death, they sold for only a fraction of the homey small-town slices of American life he was famous for. Take away the squeaky-clean image of Mary Tyler Moore or Doris Day, and what's left? Just another tired Hollywood scandal that no one really wants to hear."

"Well, I have to make the effort. Did your father keep records of his independent operation?"

"He was anal about it, but I'm the only one who knows about them; otherwise the courts would have seized them for evidence. I've got some cartons in storage. I can't see where they could hurt him now. You can take a look if you like."

Valentino remembered there was coffee left in his mug. It was lukewarm. He wondered why this son of a pornographer was being so helpful. Aloud he said, "I'd like."

13

The storage facility was, like most such establishments, located in a section of town characterized by old houses in need of repair with rooms advertised for rent, bail bondsmen's offices, adult bookstores, and businesses that cashed checks in return for a steep piece of the action. Why people chose to store their possessions in such neighborhoods was one of those mysteries even someone who promoted himself as a "film detective" was at a loss to solve.

Accompanying Hennessey there in the Candy Box van, from which the backseat had been removed to make room for cameras and sound equipment, Valentino wondered again why his host was being so cooperative with a stranger. Aloud he said, "Thanks so much. I was afraid you'd be more reluctant."

"I'm not ashamed of what my father did. In those days the people who made the business what it is — writers, house directors, and cameramen — were treated like coolies. The studios paid the absolute minimum. The poor suckers reported to work before sunup and went home past midnight without being paid a cent of overtime. Even after the unions got a foothold, the bosses found ways around the agreements they'd signed themselves. If anyone should blush over their past mistakes, it's them. Some of the people Dad worked with did a lot worse things to make ends meet."

He had to ask. "We just met. For all you know I'm one of them."

"I Googled you after you called. You found *Greed* and the test footage Lugosi shot for *Frankenstein,* before he bailed out of the production. You could have sold either one and retired, but you turned them over to UCLA for modest finder's fees and pumped every penny into a renovation project that will likely never earn you a dime. I hope you'll take this the right way, but you and Dad would have understood each other."

"I wish you'd explain that to my secretary. She thinks I'm ripping off the university just by reporting to work."

"I get the same thing from my son. He's in film school, studying the same stuff I shoot, only with subtitles."

They parked on gravel before one of a string of hangar-like buildings with garage-type doors. Vans similar to theirs, some pickups, and a pair of tractor-trailer rigs shared the lot with, incongruously, a sleek red convertible with its top down. The interior was unoccupied.

Hennessey noticed it, too. "Sign of the times, and incidentally of the place we live. Grandma's junk clashes with their flashy lifestyle, so it goes out of sight till they can sell it on Craigslist."

He sprang open a padlock with a key, slid up the door with the aid of counterweights, and activated rows of fluttering fluorescents mounted to the trusses that supported the roof. The space beneath was stacked with cartons, cardboard tubes like the ones rolled posters came in, light stands, furniture, and — presumably — motion picture props. A slinky construction of green sequins ending in a grotesque leering papier-mâché head hung from overhead cables, awaiting some future Chinese New Year's.

"Peking Tom," Hennessey said, tracking the path of Valentino's gaze. "One of our biggest draws. We're shooting the sequel on location in Mexico."

His guest said nothing. He'd lived in L.A.

too long to question non sequiturs.

"That's Dad's stuff, in those boxes. He had everything on safety stock, so storing it in a climate-controlled environment wasn't crucial."

Together they sorted through the contents of the stacked cartons. Twenty minutes in, Valentino lifted out four flat film cans bound together with twine. Faded black hand-printed letters were splayed across the can on top: A.M.

The date that followed the initials roughly corresponded with the year Valentino's father was born.

Agnes Mulvaney: Dixie Day's real name.

He slid off the twine, set down the rest of the stack, and pried the lid off the one on top. Inside was a reel of film, which Valentino removed, unwound two feet of the glittering stock, and held it up to the light. He came to the end of the countdown frames and read the title aloud:

JOHNNY TREMAIN

"Not the title you'd expect of a porno," Hennessey said.

"Not unless Walt Disney shot it," said Valentino.

He unspooled just enough more footage

to determine it was a movie about a heroic drummer boy serving in the American Revolutionary War, returned it to its can, and checked the others.

"Under other circumstances, I'd be excited." He closed the last can. "A lot of these color films on safety stock are deteriorating faster than the older two-strip classics on silver nitrate. From the looks of it, this print is intact, maybe the only pristine copy of this title in existence. I hope you'll store it properly. UCLA will be in touch."

"But it's not what you're looking for."

Valentino hadn't told him the real reason for his mission; too many people knew about it already. "I'm afraid not. Someone has made a substitution."

"We can look at the rest."

"I'm sure it's gone. Frankly, I was surprised when these cans showed up. There's evidence someone has gotten hold of the film I'm looking for, and is using it for his own purposes. When was the last time you checked out this facility?"

"It's been months; years since I took a complete inventory. That would be when I was packing the stuff up. I'm the only one at Candy Box who knows about this place. But anyone can pick a padlock." Hennessey put his hands on his hips and glanced around. "I wonder what else is missing."

"Nothing, probably. Whoever broke in was after one thing and one thing only. Probably it happened not long after you brought the stuff here. This isn't the first time it's surfaced."

"This doesn't have anything to do with negotiating for a legitimate film, does it?"

He considered continuing with the story; but the man had been up-front with him. "Not really. I'm afraid I can't be any more specific."

"You don't have to be, if what I suspect is true. I meant what I said about the difference between peddling dirty movies and extortion. If it's a blackmailer you're after, count on me for anything you need."

"You've already been a tremendous help. I had to know it was more than a bluff. So far all I've seen is blowups of frames, which can be faked. A complete motion picture, not so much. Now all I have to do is find out who had access to it."

"I'll take a lie detector test, if it'll help; my crew, too. I've worked with all of them for years, but if it helps to eliminate —"

"I believe you. You could have refused to see me, or had me thrown out of the building the minute you found out what I wanted."

132

"Maybe I just wanted to look like I was cooperating."

"That'd be too clever. California has almost as many blackmailers as film technicians; I've run into a few even in my line. Criminal geniuses they're not."

"I guess not, but why would this one bother to switch out the films instead of just taking Dad's?"

"Maybe he wanted to buy time before you discovered it was missing."

Hennessey shook his head. "I didn't exactly take exhaustive inventory when I moved this stuff here, but I know my father never worked for Disney. The burglar had to have brought it with him."

"You mean as a sort of apology for the theft? That would be a new one."

"Maybe it was his only one."

"An amateur with a conscience?" It was Valentino's turn to shake his head. "That doesn't agree with anything I know about blackmailers."

"So now you've got two mysteries on your hands."

"When I solve the one, the other should solve itself." He held out the stack of cans with some reluctance; surrendering motion picture treasures didn't come naturally to him. "You've done me such a favor, I hesitate to ask if you'd consider selling this print to UCLA before offering it anywhere else."

"And deal with Disney's lawyers? Thanks, but I prefer to work with porn stars. If you can come to an agreement with them over the rights, I'd appreciate it if you'd insert a credit line in memory of Dick Hennessey."

The pair grasped hands.

There was no sign of the red convertible when they pulled out of the parking lot; but Valentino caught a glimpse of it in the mirror on his side of the van when they turned the last corner before the studio where he'd left his car. He couldn't see anything of the driver through the heavily tinted windshield. He pointed it out to his companion, who looked up at the rearview. "I doubt I'd know him if I got a good look at him. I don't travel in that kind of circle. I still owe sixteen more payments on this old rattle-trap."

They were slowing near the studio when the car turned into a side street.

"Coincidence, I guess," Hennessey said. "Then again, there are more red sports cars in Southern California than melanomas. Anyway, the one we saw was at the storage place before we were."

"You're right. If the driver's interested in us he has to be clairvoyant, in which case why follow us at all?"

They parked and got out of the van. "Good luck with the bloodsucker," Hennessey said.

The film archivist grinned. "Are you talking about blackmailers or the Disney legal department?"

"Both."

Valentino thanked him again, carried his new prize to his car, and drove back to the office. The convertible was parked almost in front of the door.

■ ■ ■ ■ ■

II
OATER

■ ■ ■ ■ ■

14

He channeled every sleuth he'd ever seen, from William Powell's jaunty operative in the inexplicably titled *Private Detective 62* through the Burt Reynolds rip-off of Bogart's *The Big Sleep* in *Shamus;* but unlike the old days, automobiles no longer came with convenient labels strapping the owners' registrations to the steering columns, and the glove compartment that usually contained such information today was locked. He was about to give it up as the stuff of real detectives when he spotted what was missing: There were no pedals for acceleration or braking. Extra levers had been added to the steering column, designed to serve those who hadn't the use of their lower extremities.

He knew then, beyond a reasonable doubt, who belonged to the snazzy set of wheels.

From there he schlepped the stack of cans to the university's high-tech lab, where the attendant knew where to store them without instruction.

Smith Oldfield's office next. The tweedy transplanted New England attorney was out at the time, but Valentino left specific instructions with his legal secretary, a steely efficient woman who'd placed third runner-up in the Miss Barstow Beauty Pageant, as to what he required.

When he checked in at his own office, Ruth told him he had a visitor waiting for him inside.

"I expected as much," he said. "I could even provide a description. Give me one good reason why I shouldn't change the lock. For all you know, anyone could walk in there and walk out with everything he needed to benefit our competitors."

"Not if he tried to walk it past me. I once tackled a pirate from Columbia sneaking an advance copy of *Duel in the Sun* out of David O. Selznick's office."

"You're old, Ruth, but you're not *that* old. Try not to make yourself out as a sex-changed Dorian Gray."

"Well, it might have been something else, from somebody else's office. The point is, as long as I'm around, locks are redundant.

"Anyway," she added, picking up a pair of headphones likely attached to Kyle Broadhead's latest dictation, "Who says I'm old?"

"All I know is I saw someone who looked a lot like you in a woodcut Hieronymus Bosch made in 1510."

But he waited until she was listening to the tape before he said it.

The woman he found sitting behind his desk would, in thirty years or so, bear a close resemblance to the dragon in reception. She was lithe, almost rangy, wore her black-black hair shellacked close to her skull, and had turned out today in a trim black sheath with a spiral of scarlet thread twirled about it like the stripe on a barber pole. He couldn't fail to note that the color matched her sports car exactly, and wondered if she coordinated her outfit with the transportation or the transportation with the outfit on a daily basis. Considering the way her employer, Mark David Turkus, flung money around when it came to running Supernova International, he wouldn't be surprised if it were the latter.

"You won't find anything worth looking at in my desk, Teddie," he said, seating himself in the chair opposite. Moving the stack of vintage movie magazines from the cushion was less cumbersome than evicting her from his swivel. Anyway, from the arrangement of her automobile controls and the aluminum crutches leaning against the wall inside her reach — painted glossy red, of course — the prospect struck him as inhumane.

As inhumane as she was.

"The computer, either," he added. "You can even have the password if you want. I stopped trusting sensitive information to cyberspace last year, after a hacker maxed out my credit card at Target."

"I wouldn't think of pawing through this rat's nest you call a workstation," she said in her purring whisper. "And I seldom use a computer. Why bother? I remember every joke I've ever been told and my private life is more interesting than pornography."

He didn't doubt her. Teddie Goodman would stop at nothing, including seduction, to procure lost film footage for her boss. She'd cribbed the act, as well as her name, from Theda Bara, whose silent-screen *nom de travail* sounded more exotic than Theodosia Goodman from Ohio. For years now, then, it had been the Vamp vs. the Sheik, with Teddie and Valentino racing each other to prize after prize; he for the sake of posterity, she for the sake of Turkus' generous finder's fees.

"I thought you'd be off the crutches by now." He was genuinely concerned, as well as racked with survivor's guilt. She'd been thrown down the stairs from the projection booth at The Oracle by thugs searching his theater for the same reels she'd been looking for herself.

"Complications, dear. I've had six surgeries. Fortunately I have a high threshold of pain, as well as a honey of a company health-insurance plan."

"Nice car," he said, changing a subject that if he expressed his feelings on it would only arouse her sense of weakness on his part. "Gift from the Turk?"

"He offered to hire me a limo until I can drive myself, but I said it would just slow me down. He couldn't have that, of course. He went personally to the factory in Rome to oversee the custom work. It was in the way of a bonus for *A Star Is Born*."

"I heard about that. You tracked down the courting scene from the Judy Garland version without leaving your bed in Mount Sinai. That was impressive."

"You think so only because you weren't on its trail at the time."

Which robbed you of some of the triumph, he thought; but he tried as much as possible not to be catty when in conversation with her. She was feline — no, leonine — enough for both of them; and, although he'd never acknowledge it, he felt a grudging respect for her instincts. He really believed she'd rather outsmart a reluctant possessor of something her master coveted than "vamp" it out of him. That would be the last resort — not because of any sense of integrity or aversion to the sordid, but because she was a hunter. Valentino doubted she held the cinema in any regard more lofty than loot. It was just that she knew more about it than any person living, except perhaps Kyle Broadhead, and a lioness always keeps to her home ground, enjoying the chase and then the kill at least as much as the feast that followed.

Which was why she must never know what she already more than suspected, that he'd have done what she did for nothing but the pure love of preserving the only history he really cared about. Sense his weakness? No; *smell* it, like the beast of prey she was.

But he hadn't her passion for the game, only what it brought to the UCLA Film Preservation Department, and so curiosity got the better of him. "How'd you know I'd be at the storage facility? I didn't know myself until I caught a ride."

She shifted in his chair, paling briefly at some pain that managed to cross her threshold, then found a position that seemed to please her; needless to say, it was catlike.

"I'm secure enough in my skills not to pretend it wasn't an accident. Mark sent me there to inspect one of the fountains Jean Negulesco had made for *Three Coins;* he bought it at auction ten years ago, when his current wife was blowing out the candles on her sixteenth birthday cake, and stuck it away until he made the mistake of showing her a picture. He's redoing that ghastly chalet he built in Carmel — I should say re-redoing it, as he remodels every time he remarries — and his child bride thinks it would be just the thing for the foyer. Functional, of course. The excavation and installation of drain tiles alone will approach the amount of his most recent settlement. However, when I caught sight of you alighting from that *Munsters* van, I decided to postpone the errand and see what you were up to. I knew where you'd be headed, so I drove straight here. What was in those cans I saw you carrying out?"

"You must have hightailed it around the corner after you saw it. Your car wasn't there when we pulled out."

"You were too busy hugging those cans to your chest to see me getting into the car. You know, Val, I'd admire to get you in a game of strip poker sometime. I'd have you down to your hide in three hands."

He shuddered inwardly at the image. There was nothing sexual in it, just the picture of a man being skinned alive.

"There's no reason to keep it a secret, Teddie. When I figured out you belonged to the convertible I ran them over to the lab for safe storage until Smith Oldfield in Legal decides how to approach Disney concerning rights. It looks to be a pristine print of *Johnny Tremain,* with no bleeding or fading in the color."

She pouted — not, in her case, an expression of disappointment, but of a professional deep in thought. From her cleavage she excavated a cobalt-blue marvel the size and thickness of two playing cards (six months Valentino's salary right there), rattled her crimson nails on the keys, and flicked her fingers at the screen. Red embers glowed in the centers of her coal-black irises as she read the scroll. At length she switched off the gadget and returned it to its secure place.

"Not on my list. Sanitized American history isn't one of Mark's interests, and one of his ambitions is to buy Walt Disney's frozen carcass, thaw it out in his microwave, and serve it to the CEO of Pixar at a barbecue.

"But of course you'd know that," she added.

Here he was on safe ground. He reached across the desk and scooped his telephone receiver off its cradle. "I'll call Oldfield and ask him to arrange a screening. You can talk to him yourself to discuss a convenient time. I'm sure the Turk is anxious to learn the condition of the latest Mrs. Turkus' toy."

He felt bad about that after she left, swinging out on her crutches and disdaining his offer to help her; but at the time, it was a victory.

God help him when she found out what Johnny Tremain was drumming up behind the scenes.

15

At the end of an adventurous — and largely
uninformative — day, Valentino checked in
by phone with Harriet, who was working on
a case involving what she called a "compromised corpse"; meaning one so decomposed
even its gender was open to question. She
seemed about to provide details when he
said good night. Exhausted, he slid grate-
fully between the sheets of his rollaway bed
in the projection booth. The phone rang.

"Mr. Red Montana calling for Mr. Valentino." The male voice, although youthful,
might have belonged to Franklin Pangborn,
the middle-aged, prissy hotel clerk in every
old movie.

Instinctively, Valentino fell back on his
best grammar. "This is he."

"I'm Michael Van Zendt, Mr. Montana's
personal assistant. He wishes to —"

There was a fumbling noise on the other
end while the receiver changed hands and

Montana's deep, somewhat phlegmy baritone came on. His drawl was broader than usual; marinated, the archivist concluded, in what the old cowboy would call firewater.

"Just thought I'd reel in some kind of progress report." Ice cubes collided on his end, confirming the suspicion.

"None yet." Valentino patted back a yawn. "If it means anything, I've eliminated Slap O'Reilly and the man who produced the porno."

"It's a start; though I wouldn't count out Slap just yet. He's got a mean hate on me; gratitude's the rarest flower that grows in the Great American Desert." Cubes jingled, the golden throat worked twice audibly, ending in an *aaah!* "I'm hoping you and your cute little filly might oblige me with that tour of my basement. I ain't offering the stuff for sale, so the world won't likely see it till Ol' Red's dead. That's when the Smithsonian'll start sniffin' around. Ain't nothing like a dirt bath to wash you in the blood of the lamb for that egghead crowd."

Valentino drew out another yawn he didn't really need, stalling for thought. The prospect offered much to the movie enthusiast, but little to his quest; then again, anything that broadened understanding was ostensibly of use.

What the heck. The last great cowboy star was offering him a special look at the items that had placed him in that spot.

"What time?"

A moment while the King of the Range consulted his Red Montana Rolex. "How's about seven tomorrow? I ain't missed a sunrise since they split open my chest last year."

After agreeing, Valentino called Harriet. She sounded harried.

"I have to ask you to make it fast, Val. I'm up to my elbows in ripe intestines."

From instinct, he let the receiver dangle between thumb and forefinger and informed her of the invitation.

"Tempting; but at seven a.m. tomorrow my fondest hope is I'll be busy raising blisters on the ceiling above my bed, snoring like a longshoreman."

"I happen to know you purr like a kitten," he said. "But I understand. Maybe he'll give you a raincheck, and another free pass in the gift shop."

"Wouldn't that be nice! I've turned down five offers to buy that silver bracelet off my wrist; one from a lieutenant with Homicide who's never been married nor been seen with a woman on his arm. The stories I could tell you . . ."

"But you'd have to kill me."

"In this town?" There was a nasty sound in the background of wherever she was; as if he didn't know. "I've got to hang up now. The intern I stole from Special Investigations just threw up."

"Stop sweet-talking me," he said, and let her get back to work.

It was one of those breathtaking sunrises artificially enhanced by the toxins in the air — what the locals called an L.A. particular — with bold broad slashes of orange, green, purple, and yellow that made him itch for his pastels before he realized he wasn't an artist. Against that backdrop, Red Montana's arched back, upraised arm, and trusty mount working catlike miracles with its spine looked like a Remington painting, or rather a color slide shot by a master photographer, coursing hot blood through the veins of a sculpture in bronze. Valentino hoped someone would find a home for the statue rather than let it be smelted into a panel on a celebrity's private jet.

The huge parking lot was empty; a sight that sank his heart. Not so much as a tumbleweed drifted across it. In six months at the outside, the site would host a shopping center or a high-end golf course or more likely — property values being what they were here in the rapidly shrinking vastness of the American West — one of those housing developments where the homes blooped out of a massive eye-dropper as in a factory scene in a Tex Avery cartoon.

Montana himself was standing in front of the museum entrance when he pulled up, thumbs hooked inside his broad silver-studded belt with a square buckle the size of an ashtray; embossed with his image aboard Tinderbox in full buck, of course. From a little distance, his disproportionate height — four-inch bootheels, obvious lifts, shortish legs, average trunk, and immaculate white ten-gallon hat with its tall crown — made him look like Yosemite Sam on stilts.

Valentino shook his head, clearing it of disrespectful images. He was in an animation frame of mind, it seemed. Red was just staying true to his image, in a vintage Nudie suit tailored to his frame when it was made and expertly altered as nature itself altered the frame, sky-blue with Swarovski crystals scripting his name across the yoke. A longhorn skull emblazoned with what were most likely diamonds snugged his bolo tie up to his ropy throat. From hat to hand-lasted heels, he was wearing a month's worth of restoration work on The Oracle.

"Leave 'er there, son," he said, when Valentino braked. "You won't be towed. I sent Pat Garrett and the posse packing. Not many folks get to see a real-live ghost town in the making."

His guest made excuses for Harriett; his host's disappointment was lechery incarnate. Valentino shifted to a safer subject. "What will happen to the place?"

"I got an offer from one of them pimple-faced dot-com skillionaires who's fixing to turn it into a stadium for an expansion team. Lacrosse, maybe; anyway one of them games more fun to play than watch. I'm thinking of having 'em call it the Dixies or no deal. What do you think?"

"You could suggest an MVP award at the end of the season." Valentino grinned. "The Dixie Cup."

The famous Red Montana grin turned his multiple chins into a concertina and made him glow all the way to the spurs he wasn't wearing. Valentino braced himself, but the palm that smacked his back sent him reeling anyway.

"Son, I wisht you was born fifty years ago. You'd of made that sidewinding S.O.B. Slap O'Reilly look like the spear-carrier he was born to be. No sense of humor, that was his whatchacall Killer's Heel. He made folks laugh, right enough; but anybody can raise a snicker tripping over his own feet and falling face-first into a pile of cowflop. I told him he'd of been as big as the Marx Brothers if the cows just ate more and learned to crap on cue."

His guest's grin faded to a feeble smile. He wondered just how many LED bulbs for The Oracle his Red Montana costume would finance at auction. It was fast losing value for him.

The tour, however, was worth the early hour, and very nearly worth his diminishing regard for his host.

The basement storage area ran the length and width of the building, illuminated by halogen bulbs in ceiling canisters that came on in succession as Montana flipped switches spaced along the walls. The walls themselves were painted industrial white, so that when all the lights were burning not a square inch was left in shadow. They passed among rack after rack of costumes, each tagged with the name of an actor or actress whose name was familiar to Valentino; he could feel the presence of Hoot Gibson, Jane Russell, Noah Beery, Joanne Dru, Jay Silverheels, Hattie McDaniel, and dozens more of his heroes since childhood inhabiting the clothes.

"You didn't work with all these people," he said.

"Just a few; some were dead or retired before I started. You hang around a place as long as me, you gather stuff. Some of it comes to you all on its own, like this here." He fingered the sleeve of a man's drab coat, soiled, shapeless, and missing most of its buttons. "Guess who it belonged to."

The style was reminiscent of old sepia photographs Valentino had seen in history books. "Some old prospector?"

"William Barclay Masterson."

"*Bat* Masterson? But he was a dandy!"

"You don't think he posed for pictures dressed in this. A feller lent it to me to protect my clothes when I was scouting an abandoned mineshaft for *Colorado Rag*. I clean forgot to give it back. I was getting set to throw it out when I put my hand in a pocket, like you do in case there's something worth holding on to. This here's what I found."

From a side pocket of the old coat he drew a scrap of paper, falling apart at the folds with the printing and pencil scribble faded almost to invisibility. It read:

A-1 CELESTIAL LAUNDRY
W.B. Masterson, $0.75
13-1-81

"See that line through the seven?" Montana asked. "That's usually the mark of a foreigner, also writing the day of the month before the number of the month, backwards from the way an American does it. It took me months to confirm that Masterson was in Houston, Texas the first part of 1881; there wasn't an Internet when I done my research. By sheer dumb luck in a book in my own liberry I came across a picture taken of the place in '79, and there smack dab on the main drag was a sign that said 'Celestial Laundry.' Back then when you wanted a good wash you went to the Chinese."

"I don't know if it's dumb, but you sure had luck."

"Can't count on it all the time. I spent a bundle on most of the rest."

The tour continued among vintage firearms, including several rifles decorated with brass tacks — "Indian weapons, probably Cheyenne," explained the actor. "They liked to gussy 'em up with doodads they got in trade." He pointed out the stamped letters on the receiver plates: HARPERS FERRY.

There were movie scripts stacked neatly on metal utility shelves, rows and rows of cowboy hats and boots, an assortment of whips — Montana identified which had belonged to bullwhackers and which to muleskinners — a gallery of posters reaching back to the earliest days of silent westerns; a dizzying array. At times his host strode so swiftly Valentino had to lope to keep up. From time to time they lingered before an item of particular interest to the owner. He lifted a handsome Colt revolver from inside the velvet-lined case in which it was displayed. It had a stag handle, yellow with age, and was plated with shiny metal.

"Sterling silver. I don't let nobody polish it but me." With an expertise that belied the age spots on his hands, Montana executed a neat border roll, ending with the buttplate facing his guest and the engraving: W.S.H. TO J.M., 1946.

"I ain't been able to make up my mind whether to will this to somebody or have it buried with me."

Anticipating what came next, Valentino said, "I'm going to take a wild stab and say the first set of initials belong to William S. Hart."

"A cigar for the lad. What about the second?"

After flipping through his mental rolodex, he let his mouth drop open. "Not — ?"

"Yep. Joel McCrea. Bill Hart gave it to him just a few weeks before he died. Joel give it to me in 1990, just before *he* cashed in. He offered to add my initials, but there wasn't no more room on the plate and I said it'd be a shame to scratch up fine silver just for me. It's just about the most valuable thing I own, and it didn't cost me a cent. Here." He held it out for Valentino to take.

The film archivist's heart leapt; but after he'd held the artifact a moment, feeling its weight, Montana held out his hand for its return.

"Not just yet, son. Check back when I'm on my deathbed."

Before they left, however, the aging icon paused before something gleaming on the wall, then lifted it from its hook and turned it Valentino's way. It was a bright yellow disk some ten inches square, framed in glass, with a brass plate containing the same title printed on its round paper label, with additional information:

COLUMBIA RECORDS
Dancers in the Dawn
from
The Republic Pictures Presentation
"In Old Dakota"
Performed by
"Red" Montana
and the Texas Wranglers
1,000,000 copies sold

"My first gold record," he said. "Hell, my first *record*. Who'd-a-thunk a Nebraska boy, still wet behind the ears, would be heard by more folks than he ever expected to meet in a hunnert years?" He held it out.

"I can't —"

"You'd be doing me a favor, son. I don't want to see it show up in some yard sale in Ensenada."

He fingered the gift, wondering if eBay would bring enough from it to reglaze the candy counters in The Oracle.

Which was the kind of thinking that had made Montana what he was. Somewhere out there, he heard Teddie Goodman's cynical snicker.

He returned it. "Thank you for the thought, but if anything comes of our arrangement, it might be misconstrued as an inducement."

Montana's face went dead. He returned the item to its hook. "I wish I could get your measure. You can trust a dishonest man to be what he is, but whenever I meet a body who don't want nothing for himself, I reach back to make sure my wallet's where I left it."

He thumped a manicured nail against Valentino's chest. "Get me that blackmailing skunk. If you don't have a name next time I hear from you, next thing you'll see is a big plume of smoke over this here building. That'll be *Sixgun Sonata* going up in flames."

16

"Tell him to take a long walk off a shorthorn steer," Harriet said, "or however they put it out on the plains. From what you've told me about how careless this business has been in protecting its product, there are plenty of other lost films in the world."

Valentino nodded over his breakfast. "Granted; with some reservations as to the sense of the last statement. If they're lost, are they still in the world?"

"If you insist on educating me this early, I'll give you the blow-by-blow on last night's autopsy."

They were dining in the Brass Gimbal, ordinarily the private haunt of Valentino and Kyle Broadhead; but although he needed a sounding board, the film archivist was reluctant to face his mentor until he'd made some inroads on the guest list for the bachelor party. What calls he'd managed to squeeze in between rummaging through the late Dick Hennessey's legacy and jousting with Teddie Goodman had borne no fruit beyond a roster of the deceased. (One promising lead, a former researcher for Cecil B. DeMille, turned out to have died in a rollover accident involving a camel while vacationing in the Valley of the Kings.)

As always, the establishment was only half full in the middle of the morning rush. Every visit, it seemed, turned up fewer patrons with an interest in the technical side of the industry: Framed signed photos of such pioneers as Harry Rubin, Herbert Griffin, and the Lumiere brothers appealed only to a particular description of cinema geek; how many people knew or cared who refined the modern motion-picture projector, brought the canals of Venice to the Hollywood soundstage through the genius of the process shot, invented the technique known as movie magic? Most people only took notice of the nuts and bolts when the theater screen went mute and they pounded the floor with their feet, shouting for sound. Every day the Gimbal managed to open its doors was another day wedged between it and the establishment of L.A.'s one hundred thousandth Starbucks.

Valentino had ordered an item identified on the menu as the United Artists Special, comprising the Chaplin and the Fairbanks, garnished with the Mary Pickford; which for all the world tasted like ordinary scrambled eggs and ham with sweet gherkins. Harriet's "Uncle Carl," at least, seemed more worthy of its namesake, the five-foot tall Carl Laemmle, founder of Universal Pictures: a short stack smothered in syrup and seasoned with paprika.

He'd told her just enough of his arrangement with Red Montana to make her bristle at the man's arrogant bullying, holding back the blackmail angle, partly in deference to his "client's" wishes, partly out of respect for Dixie Day's reputation.

Sudden, sinking sensation: Would the Sweetheart of the Range turn out to be as much of a disappointment in person as her spouse?

He shook his head, as much to rid himself of the feeling as to respond to Harriet's threat to lay out the details of her overnight session with a cadaver *in extremis*. "To be honest, I'd consider that a relief after the things I've learned. I always knew there was a cesspool under the Dream Factory, but I'm beginning to feel it lapping at my pants cuffs."

"Then step out of it. Do you really think civilization will come to an end if there's one less oater in it?"

He blinked. "Yes."

They ate some more in silence. A waiter dressed like an old-time usher, pillbox cap and all, came by, freshened Valentino's coffee, and swapped a fresh pot of hot water for Harriet's tea. When he drifted off:

"Well, maybe civilization will go on, but I'm not sure I'd want to be part of it if I didn't do all I could to rescue something that's so nearly inside my grasp. I couldn't walk away from it any more than I could turn my back on an innocent animal that's headed for the gas chamber."

"They don't use gas anymore. I opened up a Humane Society attendant who took a dose of what they're shooting into them now: methylene blue and chloral hydrate, with a cyanide chaser. What the sports in the kennels call a Mickey Mouse Finn." She looked up from her forkful of Uncle Carl to meet his gaze. "Sorry. I'm a little punchy. I was sliding between some cool and lovely sheets when someone called inviting me to breakfast."

"Now *I'm* sorry. I'm not asking for a solution, just a sympathetic ear."

"You came to the wrong person. I provide solutions for a living."

She chewed, swallowed, sipped tea, clicked

the cup into its saucer, and pushed her plate away to fold her arms on the table. When her face was solemn she was incredibly beautiful: Garbo in close-up, expertly filtered, with eyes as big as planets. Then she spoiled it by going into a yawn that almost cracked her face.

She patted her mouth, shook herself. "Sorry. I really have to get some sleep, but before I stick you with the check, I'll leave you with one thought."

He braced himself. "Shoot."

"You've loved movies all your life, no?"

"No. I mean yes." He hated it when she cross-examined him.

"Has it ever occurred to you to ask if they've ever loved you back?"

The usher drifted back their way, paused infinitesimally, then drifted off, propelled by an instinct as old as his profession.

Valentino blew air. "That sounds like something Kyle would say."

"How is the old buzzard?"

"Feathering his nest."

"His and Fanta's has to be the most bizarre coupling since Wallace Beery and Gloria Swanson."

He smiled. "You've been doing your Hollywood homework. I told you before you don't have to butter me up. I like you just as much when you talk about spatter patterns and bone saws."

She unfolded her arms and reached across the table to take his hand in both of hers. "Such a sweet talker. Now take me out of here and tuck me in. Everything will look so much better in the morning."

"It *is* morning."

"Is it?" She looked blearily out the bright window. "I thought they were going a little heavy on the neon."

He was still in need of counseling, and prepared to undergo Kyle Broadhead's particular brand of catechism in order to receive it.

It would go, he predicted, thus:

Kyle, I think we have to face the fact that most of the people you want to wish you well on your marriage have passed.

Passed? You mean I'm being boycotted?

No, I mean they're no longer with us.

They seldom are. At any given time, they're digging up dinosaur bones in Utah, tracking the origins of Sanskrit in Calcutta, scraping bits of bronze off Doric weaponry on Minos, attempting to determine —

Dead! Kyle, they're all dead! You've managed to outlive everyone who could serve as a pallbearer at your own funeral.

166

Well, isn't that the point?

Or something along those lines. Father Broadhead never dispensed absolution without exacting a price for the service.

Valentino took a deep breath and knocked on Kyle's office door. The voice that invited him to enter lacked the film scholar's world-weary rasp. It was a smooth contralto; the kind that made even a man committed to a monogamous relationship tingle to the soles of his feet.

Fanta, the professor's bride-to-be, sat on the corner of the sacred desk, her gypsy skirt hiked up above one polished knee. With it she wore a white peasant blouse off the shoulders and a tiny emerald on a thin gold chain around her long neck, its iridescent green matched to her eyes. Her blue-black hair, caught above one temple with a clasp of some kind, spilled over the opposite shoulder nearly to her waist. She was a breathtaking twenty.

Why, the visitor wondered, did no one ever speak of a brunette as "willowy"? The adjective seemed exclusive to blondes, and yet he could think of no better word to describe the lithe flexibility of her tall frame.

"Hello, Val. Kyle's teaching class, so I thought I'd take the opportunity to rifle his desk. I found these in that funny compartment where they used to keep ledgers." She indicated a stack of green cardboard sleeves violating the compulsive tidiness of Broadhead's desk. The one on top was empty. She read aloud the label on the ten-inch-wide black disc she was holding. " 'Jeannine.' That was his first wife's name. I suppose it would be wildly inappropriate to play it at our wedding."

"You suppose right."

"A shame. I seem to remember the song, from a movie Kyle played once in class." She hummed a snatch: *Jeannine, I dream of lilac time . . .* She looked up from the label. "What's a seventy-eight?"

"His generation's equivalent of a CD. A buzz saw turns a little faster." He looked at the date on his watch. "What's he doing teaching? It isn't the last Friday of the month."

"Not my idea. I think he has some idea of impressing me with his newfound dedication. You know, supporting the little wifey. Never mind that I've got a standing offer to join Preston and Preston the minute I pass the bar, with a salary starting at —"

"Please," he said. "I'm depressed enough."

She flicked a glance at him, then returned the record to its sleeve and the sleeve to its stack. She slid off the desk, adopting a more formal pose leaning against it with arms crossed. "Would you like to talk about it? I'm working on my listening skills."

He started to shake his head, then realized he'd seated himself in the chair facing the desk, like a penitent in a confession booth. He began talking then. She listened without interruption or expression. At a crucial point he hesitated.

"You're not my attorney, but can I count on your confidence?"

"Val, it's Fanta. Do I have to remind you how we met?"

The circumstances had been the same as when he'd first locked eyes on Harriet Johansen. Then, the poised young woman standing before him had been an eager undergraduate, recently a student of Kyle Broadhead's, offering no clues to any of them that before the end of the adventure she and Valentino's mentor would be an item. Together, despite threats of incarceration and prosecution for obstruction of justice, the team had secured the rights to *Greed,* that Holy Grail of film preservationists, and incidentally solved the mystery of the forty-year-old corpse in the basement of The Oracle.

He told her everything then, including the details of Dixie Day's youthful indiscretion.

True to her legal training, and typical of her Internet-wise generation, Fanta registered neither shock nor judgment, except when she expressed bewilderment over all the fuss.

"It's so ridiculous. You can't turn on *Entertainment Tonight* without seeing a pixilated video of some public personality's sex tape. You almost have to make one to become a star."

"We've come a long way since Lana Turner was discovered sipping a soda," he said. "In Dixie's day, it *kept* you from becoming a star."

" 'Dixie's day,' ha! What did Harriet say?"

"She asked me if the movies loved me as much as I loved them."

"That sounds like something Kyle would say."

"That's what *I* said. We can't marry the same person."

But she'd stopped smiling. "If you wanted me to talk you out of what you're doing because the man you represent is bogus, you came to the wrong person. I'm studying the law, remember? It takes precedence over the character of the client, just as medicine trumps who the patient is."

"Film isn't the law or medicine. The people I deal with, living and dead, made it

170

up as they went along. There was no Hippocrates or American Bar Association to tell you what to do and how far you can go. If Montana's serious about destroying the print if I back out of our arrangement, he's as much a blackmailer as the person I'm looking for."

She changed positions, uncrossing her arms, leaning forward, and tucking her hands between her knees. They were so close he could smell her light scent, something citrusy with a dash of jasmine. Not so long ago it had been only the sharp clean tang of inexpensive soap. She'd become a woman before his very eyes.

"You're spending too much time thinking about Red Montana," she said. "The man you're working for isn't the man you grew up watching on the Western Channel; *that* Montana was a committee effort, assembled piecemeal on the line, tested in the market, and distributed retail, just like SpaghettiOs and Count Chocula. So was Dixie Day. The person you should be thinking about is — what was her real name again?"

"Agnes Mulvaney."

"She should've stuck with it. How many Dixies are there in this town, and how few Agneses? But don't stop at just thinking. Talk to her."

171

"But Montana said —"

She leaned back again, recrossed her arms, said nothing.

What a lawyer she'd make, he thought.

The door opened and Kyle Broadhead came in, wearing his standard shabby tweed uniform and something unique for him, the sharp scent of Magic Marker, the twenty-first century's answer to blackboard chalk. He hesitated when he saw them, then came forward and heaved his shabby and bulging briefcase onto the desk, toppling the stack of phonograph records across the top.

"Pardon me," he said, foraging in his various pockets for his pipe and tobacco. "I didn't mean to interrupt the sock hop." He looked at Valentino. "How you getting on with that list?"

17

He got himself out of that predicament by pleading lateness for an appointment. Kyle didn't believe him; but then he assigned incredulity to everything, so it was the same as acceptance.

The appointment was with Valentino himself, at The Oracle, where for once the mysterious disappearance of the work crew proved less an irritation than a blessing. After rummaging a while among the archives in the basement — that fabled cool, dry place where most things are supposed to be stored — he produced a quality print of the film he considered the best western ever filmed.

Up in the projection booth/cum personal apartment, he threaded the first reel onto the Bell & Howell projector, and for the next ninety-four minutes lost himself in Randolph Scott's last performance, Joel McCrea's next-to-last, ingenue Mariette

Hartley's first, and Sam Peckinpah's inaugural effort on the big screen.

Ride the High Country had not enjoyed the confidence of its studio, which had released it on the bottom half of a double bill with a feature no one now remembered; but it was an important link between the idealistic western of the old school as represented by veterans Scott and McCrea and the gritty, ultra-realistic frontier drama for which the renegade Peckinpah would soon become known through such no-holds-barred classics as *The Wild Bunch* and *The Ballad of Cable Hogue.* When the old-timers stride out to do battle old-school with grungy brothers John Anderson, Warren Oates, L.Q. Jones, John Davis Chandler, and James Drury, the American western registered the shift on the Richter scale. It would never be the same again.

Valentino entertained no pretenses toward sophistication. When, at a crucial moment, the larcenous Scott asks the straitlaced Mc-Crea, "Is that all you want?" the one-man audience perched on the edge of his seat for the response:

"All I want is to enter my house justified."

He found himself applauding the line, there alone in his own theater. John Wayne would never have gotten away with such a sentiment; only McCrea, icon of nobility that he was, could have sold it.

From Western Channel reruns of *The Lone Ranger* through the entire oeuvre of Scott, McCrea, Sunset Carson, Hoot Gibson, Tom Mix, Harry Carey, Bob Steele, James Stewart, Richard Widmark, Clint Eastwood, and so many others, Valentino's entire code of conduct had been based on these avatars of justice. It didn't matter that in the real West, survival was the object, whether one's tormentor was shot from in front or in back; the American western was the chief spokesman for the Golden Rule. It was no coincidence that the motion picture theater, so dominated by the outdoor drama, with its rows of seats facing the altar of the bright screen, resembled the interior design of a church. In the West presented by Hollywood, right was right and wrong was wrong, and the line dividing one from the other was bold and black. There were no gray areas in Texas.

Someone else clapped, with cynical pauses in between.

He switched off the projector to peer through the square opening overlooking the orchestra. There sat Teddie Goodman, twisted with an elbow over the back of her sheet-wrapped seat — the elbow sheathed,

175

as usual, in a long white glove a la Theda Bara — and her gaze fixed on the projectionist.

"Impressive," she said, "until you consider the good guy winds up dead while the bad guy's free to carry on. What message does that send?"

"Trust you to spoil a good thing, Teddie. Do you visit orphanages and set the kiddies straight on the subject of Santa Claus?"

"I would, if I'd thought of it. My father told me Santa shot himself because I was a bad girl, and that's why I wasn't getting any presents that year."

"I want to feel sorry for you, but I can't picture you having a father of any kind. How'd you get in?"

"If you're going to be such a noodge on historical accuracy, you should know that the keyhole in the front door's big enough to stick my fingers in and work the tumblers by hand."

"You can let yourself out the same way."

"What've you got going with Red Montana?"

He tried not to react. *Where did she get her information?* "I wasn't aware I had anything going with him."

"I followed you to the museum. Red met you personally in front of the building. He doesn't do that for just anyone. *Mark* can't get an interview."

"That's because even Mark David Turkus can't buy him. Red's got all the money he needs."

"And yet, curiously, he has time for a minimum-wage worker for UCLA."

"A bit more than that," he said, "but point taken. I'm curious as to why I should tell you anything. This is the second time you've entered this building illegally. The last time, someone threw you down the stairs."

"Thank you. I might have forgotten if you hadn't reminded me." She curled a set of gloved fingers over the handle of a crutch. "Look. I know what you're after; what Mark and everyone else is after when it comes to Red Montana. *Sixgun Sonata* is the only chimera connected with him, the one film no one can have because it's lost. But as you and I know, 'lost' just means no one's had the wherewithal before this to bring it to the surface. Mark has it, UCLA doesn't. Therefore, you have something to offer that Supernova International hasn't. The fact that you're here in the middle of the day watching a creaky old oater tells me you're stymied. I'm proposing a coalition: our money, your effort. You and I know that bribes must be paid. Consider the power of unlimited access."

"In return for — ?"

"Exclusive rights for Supernova to distribute *Sixgun Sonata* throughout North and South America, the European market to be negotiated later. Proceeds to be divided eighty-twenty in Supernova's favor."

"I'm not sure I can clear that with the university board of directors."

"Your partner in crime can."

Her choice of words made him wonder just how much she knew about his and Broadhead's past activities on behalf of film preservation. She was a dangerous woman.

"Fifty-fifty," he said then.

She sighed. In days of old, Theda Bara would have drawn on her cigarette holder.

"Seventy-thirty. That's as much as I was authorized."

"Even split, Teddie."

"Sixty-forty. I'm going out on a limb here."

For the first time in their relationship, Valentino knew he had Theodosia Goodman on the ropes. For whatever reason, sentimental or monetary, her employer had told her to acquire *Sixgun Sonata* at whatever the cost.

"Just so you didn't waste the trip, how about a Laurel and Hardy short?"

"Mark will never agree to fifty-fifty."

"You underestimate your powers of persuasion."

Gloved fingers twiddled the back of her seat.

"Play the one about the piano."

It won an Oscar, and also an accord: half-and-half. He told her as much as she needed to know. By then she was seated on the sofa bed in the projection booth, drinking the best he could offer, grapefruit juice from the camp refrigerator.

She set down her glass with a grimace.

"What if I told you I could deliver the surveillance video from the storage center?"

He remembered the theft of Dixie Day's video. "I don't know what it would show. The film had to have been taken years ago, when Montana was blackmailed the first time. They tape over those things again and again."

"Well, you never know. Seriously, do you not have any liquor in this dump?" She shook her glass.

"So you've made a deal with the devil," Broadhead said. "Who hasn't?"

There in the antiseptic quarters where the world's foremost authority on film held forth, that disheveled party busied himself with his pipe, twisting the stem this way and that, blowing through it, sighting down its length. He might have been preparing for some duel to the death.

Valentino snatched it from his grasp; held it in both hands across his midsection. "Sometimes I think your craving for tobacco exceeds your common sense. Did I do the right thing or not?"

Broadhead laced his fingers across his tweed waistcoat. "From the standpoint of this university, emphatically you did. Supernova can put *Sixgun Sonata* in places UCLA could never have imagined. The revenue would finance any number of acquisitions more worthy."

"So it all comes down to money."

"You needn't make it sound so sordid. Thomas Jefferson would never have agreed to the Louisiana Purchase were it not for rumors of gold in California. As it was, he bought it at a bargain, to finance Napoleon's fleet against England. Without that decision, you and I might be conducting this conversation in French. I don't know about you, but I'll never grasp their verbs."

"It's settled, then. For the first time in my career, I'm working hand-in-hand with my fiercest competitor." He returned the pipe.

Broadhead beamed. "My boy, you can't

know how happy you've made me. The first time one compromises his principles is the initial step toward maturity. One can't live in a fairy tale, even in this town."

"All I want is to enter my house justified."

"Who doesn't?" But for the first time in memory, Kyle Broadhead hadn't a speech to back it up.

Valentino watched him stuff his pipe. The professor's long tenure and international reputation gave him the privilege of invisibility when it came to the campus ban on smoking. "Harriet told me something I can't get out of my head," Valentino said. "She asked me if the movies have ever loved me back."

"It sounds like something *I'd* say."

"That's what *I* said. No one's ever caused me to question what I do before. Do you think I've been wasting my life?"

"How old are you, thirty?"

"Thirty-four. You were at my birthday party, Kyle."

"So far this year I've been to six, including Henry Anklemire's revolting one-year-old nephew's. For some reason, everyone in the world believes the anniversary of the miracle of his birth is an event worth commemorating. Fanta says if I have one more slice of nauseatingly sweet cake she'll put me on a diabetic diet. In that light, I suspect you'll forgive me if I don't keep a running account of the ages of all my acquaintances." He lit a match, but he didn't ignite his tobacco. Instead he watched the flame creeping toward his thumb and forefinger. "The point I'm getting at is I have *pipes* older than you are. My advice is to waste as much of your life as you can manage at this juncture. God knows I wish I'd wasted more of mine when I was young enough to enjoy it."

"Then you agree with Harriet."

"I never agree with women. They resent it when you do; it means you think you understand them."

"Just once I wish you'd answer a question without discussing your personal philosophy."

"*You* chose *me* to be your Yoda, remember. Do you honestly believe, because the woman you admire helps snatch the occasional murderer off the street, she's contributing more to society than you? Most homicides are committed by amateurs who will never repeat the atrocity, which renders the value of their conviction to the human race moot. Certainly it's no benefit to the victim. Every time you unearth a sparkling piece of the past, you may inspire

182

an undiscovered genius to equal something fine, even improve upon it." He blew out the match and deposited it in the metal wastebasket he reserved for that purpose.

"That sounds noble, but the last sparkling piece of the past I reassembled was a Three Stooges short called *Nyuk-Nyuk-Knuckleheads.*"

"Somewhere there's a nascent Orson Welles who'll see it and turn the act of poking one's fingers into a friend's eyes to art."

"Thanks, Kyle. I don't know if that helps."

Broadhead produced another match, this time lighting his pipe. "Don't be too hard on Harriet. Such devil's advocacy is an expression of concern. I learned that when I realized Fanta wasn't harping on my unhealthy habits out of pique."

"You don't have to tell me that. Harriet's the best thing that's happened to me since the first time my mother dropped me off at a movie matinee."

"About that bachelor party." The professor shot a stream of smoke out the side of his mouth opposite the pipe.

"I'm working on —"

"Stop working on it."

"What? Why?"

"I just got news about the fate of my oldest friend."

"I was going to tell you about that camel accident in Egypt."

"What camel accident?"

He was still trying to come up with a way out of that faux pas when his mentor resumed speaking.

"I got a call from Lou Corelli, right out of the blue. We met on the set of *Pocketful of Miracles* when I fetched cigars for Billy Wilder. He calls himself Lucille now."

"You mean — ?"

"I'm afraid so." He made a snipping motion with his fingers. "Further attempts to reach prospective guests can only add to my melancholia."

"Lucille's an isolated incident, don't you think?"

"Probably, and I don't judge. Still, the prospect of reminiscing with what is no doubt the homeliest old woman in America about the script girls we chased could trigger an attack of malaria. The likely deaths of most of the rest would deny me even that."

"You're just assuming they're dead. Look at you."

"I'm remarkably well preserved. The odds that the few doddering remnants you may manage to disinter will be pushing walkers and packing their own oxygen are such that

I'd rather not be reminded of my own approaching immolation."

"You've actually made me feel worse than when I came in."

Broadhead pointed his pipe stem north. "If it's cheerleading you're after, the Bruins are that way."

"You're infuriating."

"So I've been informed, by almost everyone I know. Now, what about this camel accident?"

Valentino left a few uncomfortable minutes later, determined now to fill out that guest list.

18

Talk to her: Fanta's words.

Red Montana had expressly forbidden him to approach Dixie Day with the blackmail investigation; but as that sharp young lawyer-to-be had indicated, the woman who'd appeared in the stag film was its center.

Valentino acted upon impulse, without even stopping at his office to arrange an appointment. Such things were easier rejected over the line than in person, and knowing himself, a moment's hesitation might kill his momentum. He pumped life into three of his four cylinders and set out for the place he considered to be the most photographed in human history.

A halo of ocher-colored smog encircled the letters of the wooden HOLLYWOOD sign as he climbed out of the L.A. basin, his temperature light flickering with each mile that separated his car from its comfort zone.

Somewhere ahead, the Montana-Day "ranch" — the Circle M— comprised fourteen acres in the Hollywood Hills, a tract that cost as much as a thousand-acre spread in Texas. The house was a rambling hacienda, ten thousand square feet of pink adobe with a red tile roof and the weathered poles that supported it sticking out the front like the spiked eyelashes of a naughty *señorita*. Red had overlooked nothing in the design.

Rocking chairs sat motionless on a front porch the length of a city block, with cactus glowering in Mexican pots on either end. The doorbell chimed the opening bars of "Friendly Camping on the Owl-Hoot Trail," the theme of the Montanas' television show. How quickly, Valentino thought, a happy tune of youth can sour. They ought to come with a freshness date.

The door swung open by the hand of a slight young woman in a crisp lime-green pantsuit. Everything about her spoke ruthless efficiency: except, the "film detective" noted, the fading streak of green in the center of her pinned-back black hair.

"I'm sorry to arrive unannounced," he said; and wished he'd worn a hat, so he could have swept it off in a gentlemanly gesture. "My name is Valentino. I'm a film archivist with UCLA. Mr. Montana knows me." He'd decided not to trade on his current mission, based on Montana's order not to do precisely what he was doing. "Is Miss Day available?"

"She's resting. She's ill." The door started to close.

Ever so gently, he pressed his shoulder against it. "Miss — ?"

"*Mrs.* Chambers. I'm her nurse. She's ill, as I said." She applied more pressure to the door. He leaned in. "I like your hair. Pretty bold for your profession."

She put a hand to her brow, an involuntary gesture, touching the pale green streak. "My last hospital was less conservative than the one I work for now. I'm growing it out."

"As if a little individual initiative would make you less efficient."

She was a trained nurse, therefore experienced with wrestling three-hundred-pound patients. The door closed despite all his pressure.

There followed several days of nothing.

Nothing, that is, on the order of either Valentino's quest for a blackmailer or for the names on Broadhead's list.

He followed one lead on the latter, which took him through a series of corporations with unenlightening names fronted by receptionists, male and female, whose inflectionless tones put him in mind of the covert agents in a Rocky & Bullwinkle cartoon, and fueled his suspicions about the professor's alleged association with nebulous intelligence agencies. (He dismissed his imprisonment in Yugoslavia in characteristically blunt fashion: "I was tracking an Eisenstein film, for heaven's sake!" Valentino was somewhat skeptical, as the specific object of Broadhead's quest seemed to keep changing.) It was the run-around of run-arounds. He'd once seen a cartoon in which a motorist puzzled over four one-way arrow signs, all pointing directly at his car.

He parried with Ruth, made a series of cold calls based on a tip involving a lost Fatty Arbuckle short, concluding in a hang-up of explosive proportions. He found that promising. The owner of an old-fashioned heavy-duty phone must have understood the value of a dollar.

There was nothing, however, to list as an accomplishment; or for that matter an expenditure of energy equal to the effort.

Nearing quitting time — five o'clock, by Ruth's Eisenhower-era standards — on Thursday, that Golem got him on the intercom.

"Some woman. Won't give her name. I'm sure you'll take it."

Before he could come up with a suitable rejoinder, Teddie Goodman's sinuous mezzo came on the line. "Our deal's still good, right?"

He remembered their conversation in that same office. "Don't tell me you found something worth looking at on surveillance."

"And they call *me* a cynic. Do you want me to say I don't? 'Cause if it's otherwise, I'm here till seven."

There'd been no reason to ask her what she'd meant by *here.* When she wasn't swooping out over one hemisphere or the other on the scent of cinematic plunder, Theodosia Goodman hung her bat wings in her seventeenth-floor office in the Capital Building, communing with the ghosts of Frank Sinatra, Dean Martin, Sammy Davis, Jr., and all the other hipsters who'd recorded with the iconic record label. The walls of the two-hundred-square-foot office were plastered with their blown-up images, gold records in frames, and nothing personal to the office's occupant. Even her desk, clear Lucite, was nearly invisible, affording the visitor a view of her long muscular legs in black nylons and narrow feet thrust into thousand-dollar black heels with red soles. The visitor was reminded of *Heat*, and thief Robert DeNiro's philosophy: nothing you can't walk away from in thirty seconds. All she had to do was snatch up her sleek crutches leaning against the desk and skedaddle.

But from *what?* She seemed to live on the edge of the nanosecond, like a hummingbird burning up every calorie it took in almost before it took it in, then flitting off to the next source of nourishment. To her, Mark David Turkus, the tenth richest man in the world (according to *Forbes*), was but a stop on the way to the ninth.

She'd dressed for the occasion, it seemed, in a suit of shimmery material that changed colors whenever she moved, like a shark sliding through waters illuminated by the tropical sun. The soles of her stiletto heels were the bright red of arterial blood.

Valentino decided it must be very exhausting to be Teddie Goodman.

"I'm surprised they let you into the building," she said by way of greeting. "Do you even *own* a necktie?"

"One, a gift to Kyle Broadhead by George Raft. I wear it to fund-raisers. You know, he taught me how to tie it."

"Broadhead? I'd have thought he wore

191

clip-ons."

"Raft. He tied his tie in front of a mirror in almost all of his movies. I ran them again and again until I got it right. I didn't know this meeting was formal. Next time I'll rent a tuxedo."

"You and Edward G. Robinson. When you want to be clever, don't quote *Double Indemnity* in front of an expert."

"I didn't know you actually watched the films you cadge. Most pirates don't spend much time studying the faces on doubloons."

"You think that's an insult. Everyone in our line of work could learn a great deal from Captain Kidd."

He threw himself into the chair facing her desk. It was upholstered in Naugahyde and shaped like a human hand: Trust his hostess to place all her visitors in her personal palm. "What've you got, Teddie?"

"Your blackmailer; or whoever he chose to front for him." She produced a slim black cylinder in a slender hand.

Directly across from her sleek desk, a rectangular screen slid down soundlessly from the ceiling, obscuring a group shot of the Rat Pack cavorting on the Las Vegas Strip. In size and scope it reminded Valentino of Oskar Werner's living room set-up in

Fahrenheit 451. As she fast-forwarded through the fuzz at the start of the video, Valentino said, "I still think anything valuable would've been taped over years ago. That's when the blackmailing began."

"Sit tight. I charmed the head of security into editing this one down to the piece that interested me."

"Don't tell me. He's written a screenplay."

"Please. My cleaning woman's written a screenplay. He thinks I can introduce him to Julia Roberts."

With a flutter, fuzz gave way to a grainy image: the front of the storage facility Valentino had visited in the company of Richard Hennessey, Jr. He recognized the number on the door. After a few jumpy moments — the facility had spared a great deal of expense in its security arrangements — a trim figure in a dark windbreaker, sweatpants, and sneakers entered the frame, glanced around like a burglar in a cartoon, spent some time on the lock on the slide-up door, and finally heaved it up. Minutes later, during which the sporadic light of a handheld flash darted about the dark interior of the storage area, the figure emerged, slid down the door, and departed without hesitation stage right. Fuzz again.

"Well?" Teddie said.

"Run it again, slower."

She rewound the tape and played it back, frame by frame. He saw then that the figure carried something under its arm; called Teddie's attention to it.

"No surprise there," she said.

"I'd expect a thief to carry something *out* of the building, not *in*."

She re-rewound and re-replayed the footage, frame by frame. Surely enough, the figure bore a bulky parcel into the storage building, to emerge moments later empty-handed.

Teddie froze the tape as the phantom set its first foot outside the enclosure. It shimmered there teasingly.

"What kind of thief leaves something behind instead of taking something out?" she asked.

For the second time in their association, Valentino felt he had the advantage. He subsided into the down-filled cushions in the hand-shaped chair, folding his hands across his spare middle with a little smile.

"A kind you'll never understand, Teddie. Can you zoom in on this shot?"

She manipulated her remote. The shadowy figure leapt forward, filling the enormous screen. From the angle, the surveillance camera appeared to have been mounted just beneath the roof, providing a view from above. The bandit's head was uncovered. The imperfect video stuttered, showing a bright green streak in a head of black hair.

"You'd think these characters would spend a little on their security equipment," Teddie said. "You can't trust the colors. It looks like the place was robbed by a Muppet."

"It does, doesn't it?"

And in that moment, he knew who the blackmailer was and where to look.

19

He asked Teddie if he could borrow the tape.

"Just remember our agreement." She pressed a button and the tape licked out of a sleek brushed-aluminum player built into the wall.

He was carrying the tape to his car when his cell rang.

"Mr. Valentino? This is Roy."

"Roy?" He flicked through his mental catalogue of acquaintances of that name. He could come up with none at present.

"Your foreman?"

He'd never considered himself the kind of person who had a foreman, but then he heard the by-now familiar whine of a circular saw in the background. The man was calling him from The Oracle. In the months and years since the beginning of that ordeal, so many contractors — plumbers, electricians, carpenters (rough and finish), painters, plasterers, layers of tile, carpet, and brick, stonemasons, glaziers, drywallers, and sundry other *ers* had marched through the crepuscular theater's echoing interior, misplacing a foreman named Roy was an understandable sin.

Roy spoke again without waiting for his existence to be confirmed. "There's a guy here says you hired him, but his name isn't on the work order and I can't reach Mr. Kalishnikov. We're not supposed to let anyone in he didn't clear."

Leo had been adamant on that point, maintaining that competitors had already absconded with a number of his original designs. *"Michelangelo had the same misfortune,"* that modest man had added. *"He threw Raphael bodily out of the Sistine Chapel."*

"Did the fellow tell you his name?" Valentino asked.

There was a fumbling sound on the other end, a muffled curse, and then a deep, virile voice came on the line. "This is Stavros. Please tell this child I'm here to turn this barn into a work of art."

"Put him back on, please." When Roy had hold of the phone again, he said, "I haven't had the chance to tell Kalishnikov about Victor Stavros. He's the woodcarver I commissioned to restore the fretwork."

"Just as long as he stays out of my men's way." The foreman hung up.

Just as Valentino hit END, the phone rang again. "Still on the job, I bet," Harriet greeted.

"I considered what you said, but —"

"I know. You can't ask a leopard to switch to stripes."

"I thought you were going home to sleep for a week."

"My phone woke me up before the alarm. The Overholts want to take us to the Argyle dining room. I said nothing doing, we'll take them; it's our turn. Okay?"

"I suppose." He still had his doubts about Laura and Evan, based on nothing more tangible than the inner sense he depended on in his work.

"Great. How's one o'clock sound?"

"Today?" He looked at the time on his screen. It was almost noon.

"Yes. The date's for lunch, and I'm disinclined to change it. I've a hunch we couldn't afford to eat there during dinner."

He'd planned another trip into the Hills, this time with evidence; but that leopard crack moved him to prove he wasn't married to his job. He said he'd pick her up.

The Argyle was a somewhat self-conscious monument to Old Hollywood, whose glamorous sylph-like platinum blondes, pencil-moustached leading men, snapbrim-wearing heavies, and city-block-length automobiles still ghosted along broad streets with historic Spanish names, making Los Angeles the most haunted town in North America. The pearlescent obelisk towered far above its horizontal neighbors on Sunset, its sloping shoulders and pinkish-white façade resembling something that Aimee Semple McPherson might have used to preach her flamboyant brand of Christianity during the Roaring Twenties. It was a hotel, but only in the sense that the Taj Mahal was a burial vault.

The lobby shimmered with black-and-white glossies in silver frames of movie goddesses in satin lounging pajamas, matinee idols in smoking jackets, and a rogues' gallery of dramatically lit gangsters, jewel thieves, and stick-up artists, all of whom looked suspiciously like Edward G. Robinson.

From the sweeping grand staircase to the sconce-lit hallways to the guest rooms, furnished with beds shaped like gondolas and balconies overlooking most of Southern California, the place seemed the result of a collaboration involving wardrobe designer Edith Head, choreographer Busby Berkeley, glamour photographer George Hurrell, and the Emperor Nero.

"This looks like just your kind of place," Harriet said. "Why haven't you taken me here before?"

Valentino cleared his throat uncomfortably. "It's a little too on-the-money. It's where producers book reclusive authors they hope to seduce out of adaptation rights to their books, impressing them with a corny show."

"It looks expensive."

"That's the other reason."

In a hushed dining room where a man in a white dinner jacket tinkled a grand piano, a tall, athletic-looking hostess in a tailored blazer with apparently no blouse underneath smiled coolly from behind her podium. Valentino, in his best sportcoat and unaccustomed necktie, felt underdressed. Harriet, wearing pleated slacks, a silk blouse, and moderate heels with her hair pinned up, looked perfectly in keeping with the posh surroundings.

"We're meeting a couple," the archivist said. "The Overholts?"

"Are you the Valentino party?"

He admitted they were.

"They asked you to meet them in Suite Sixteen-seventy-two. They thought you might like to dine with them in private."

"They must be very successful," said Valentino as they rode a mirrored elevator to the sixteenth floor, listening to a sixties pop tune over the speaker. "I couldn't afford to sleep in the lobby."

Evan Overholt answered the door. The red-haired lawyer looked comfortable in a sapphire-blue velvet jacket with a black shawl collar, gray gabardine slacks, and Italian loafers, a silk scarf knotted loosely at his throat; one of those looks only a small part of the population could pull off without inviting uncomfortable comparisons to Bruce Wayne.

"Thanks so much for coming on such short notice," he said, shaking Valentino's hand. "We're treating ourselves to the weekend for our anniversary. A babysitter became available for little Jack at the last minute, and we up-jumped-the-devil and made the reservation. We thought you'd like to help us celebrate."

"I wish you'd said something," Harriet said. "We'd have brought a gift."

"That's exactly why we didn't. Your coming here is present enough."

The sitting room was spacious, with an off-white carpet so thick the floor beneath was nothing more than hearsay, overstuffed furniture upholstered in dove-gray leather, and a sixty-inch flat-panel TV mounted above a butler's cart equipped with every type of spirit and crystal vessels to drink it from. Filmy curtains stirred in a vesper exhaling through the open French doors leading to the balcony. Multiple identical screen-printed portraits of Greta Garbo occupied a powdered-black steel frame opposite the TV. Valentino didn't have to see the signature to recognize Andy Warhol's work; and it was an original.

"Evan? Did I hear you talking to someone?" A voice Valentino recognized, from the other side of the door to what was presumably the bedroom.

"Our guests are here, dear."

"Wonderful!"

Whereupon Laura Overholt strode into the room, wearing nothing but stiletto heels and a black garter belt.

20

Six blocks from the hotel, Harriet began to laugh.

He'd never heard her laugh so hard before. The shrill noise filled the car and tears streamed down her face. He thought she was hysterical, and pulled over to try to calm her down.

Then he began to laugh just as hard.

When it was over, and they were both gasping for breath with all the windows down, he said, "Swingers! I thought they went out with fondue and water beds."

"I'll bet they have a water bed, and it's round. You should've seen your face when Laura came out of that bedroom. You looked like you were going to faint."

"I suppose we should be flattered. They said we're an attractive couple."

"Well, I'm proud of the way you handled it. Anyone else would've been a lot less polite turning them down."

It had been quite civilized. Laura, showing no embarrassment whatever, had excused herself, to return a moment later in slippers and a fluffy white robe. They'd even had a drink from the bar and discussed Evan's lack-of-progress in clearing up Victor Stavros Junior's immigration problem.

"The INS official in charge, a twerp named Spraddle, refuses even to meet with Victor Junior," Evan had said. "I suppose it's easier to treat a fellow human being like an invasive species if one never makes contact. Still, I've an idea he wouldn't change his mind if it was Mother Teresa."

"Maybe not *any*one," Valentino said to Harriet. "As couples go they're not exactly Ma and Pa Kettle."

"Were you tempted?"

"Of course not! I just wanted to get out of it in such a way that they wouldn't tell Victor Stavros Senior to quit."

"What if Evan had made a move on me? Would you have to choose between my honor and your precious motion-picture palace?"

He looked at her, resting his arm on the back of his seat. "Were *you* tempted?"

"As you said, he's not Pa Kettle."

"You're just miffed because I was right about them."

"Stop trying to show off. If you thought they had designs on our virtue, why'd you agree to meet them in a hotel suite?"

"I don't know what I thought. I just knew there was something wrong from the start. I don't know about you, but I don't make friends that easily. Where should we have lunch?" he said, changing the subject. "I'm not sure I can promise anything like what's on the Argyle's menu, but I've got a yen for a chili dog."

"Knock yourself out. I've got the day off and I'm going to spend the rest of it asleep." She yawned, then sighed, somewhat theatrically. "It never fails. Every time we manage to befriend another couple, they either split up or turn out to be perverts."

"Welcome to Los Angeles." He put the car in gear.

Valentino bought an overpriced hot dog and ate standing up in the shade of the iconic stand shaped like the entrée, then got out Kyle Broadhead's pocket-worn list of names and contact numbers and ran his finger down to the first one he hadn't crossed off. He'd skipped it previously; the exchange belonged to London, England, and he could scratch out six names in the time it took to make the connection. But he was nearing rock bottom.

After many rings he was about to hit END when a well-modulated feminine voice with a British accent said hello. It was the wrong sex; but then perhaps Lou Corelli wasn't the professor's only old chum with a Lucille trapped somewhere inside him.

"Frederick Munn is my grandfather," she said, when he'd explained himself. "*Sir* Frederick, now. He speaks of Dr. Broadhead often. They were roommates at Oxford."

"I wasn't aware Kyle attended Oxford."

"He was a Rhodes Scholar. Grandpapa says he was the first Yank he ever met. I think they were expelled the same day for setting off a plumber's rocket in the faculty loo."

No wonder he'd never mentioned it. "Is Mr. — Sir Frederick available?" He could think of no less insensitive way to determine if the man hadn't joined the vast ranks of the deceased.

"One moment, please."

More than one moment crawled past. He couldn't tell if he actually heard Big Ben chiming in the background or if the sound was just a product of his overactive imagination.

"Mr. Valentino?"

A plummy voice, dripping British upper-class. With a quickening heart, Valentino pictured it coming through a well-trimmed moustache, emphatically white. A tweedy, bowler-hat-wearing, brolly-toting, monocle-sporting sort of voice; but then Valentino's sole experience of English nobility had come to him by way of David Niven, Alan Mowbray, and C. Aubrey Smith. He confirmed his identity and asked if he had the pleasure of speaking with Sir Frederick Munn.

"*Mister,* I beseech you; until we know each other better. I only accepted the bally title out of respect for Her Majesty. It's a dashed nuisance having perfect strangers address one by his first name."

He explained his reason for calling, stringing the words together in one breath; better to hear the bad news as quickly as possible. The man would be uninterested after all these years, or unable to travel because of ill health, or too busy attending the House of Lords to spare the time.

"Nothing would please me better," the old man said. "Tell old Broadbottom Munny's on his way."

■ ■ ■ ■

III
OUTDOOR DRAMA

■ ■ ■ ■

21

For the second time that day, Valentino guided his car up past the landmark HOLLY-WOOD sign and under the redwood arch straddling the driveway leading to the Montana/Day spread. The *M* inside a circle, fashioned after the likeness of a cattle brand, was burned deeply into the wood, and towering saguaro cacti transplanted from Arizona flanked the broad curving path, its surface blazing white in sunlight reflecting off the pulverized limestone crunching beneath his tires. He remembered there had been a controversy surrounding the planting, and a substantial endowment to the state chamber of commerce in Phoenix to make the problem go away; the species at the time was headed for the endangered list after many had been poached from the Navajo reservation and public property for souvenirs and decoration.

He passed a corral, inside which a

leathery-faced trainer in overalls and a straw cowboy hat led a tall sorrel alongside the circle of whitewashed wooden fence, muscles rolling beneath its sleek coat. There was a great barn many years older than the house — moved, like the saguaros, from its original location, but with a new feature, a silhouette of the King of the Range aboard a bucking Tinderbox, cut out of tin to serve as a weathervane atop the roof. The silo that stood at one end had been painted to resemble the Thermos bottle from a Red Montana lunchbox, a bit of whimsy that made the visitor chuckle even under the burden of his purpose. Farther on stood stables, both bay doors flayed open to reveal saddles, lariats, and related tack slung from nails and resting atop the gates to the stalls. Small as it was by ranch standards, the Circle M was a working spread, breeding show horses for the equestrian trade and the occasional big-budget western.

"Dog chow too, son," Montana had confided; "though I don't let it out. When folks hear a hoss is 'put out to pasture,' I don't reckon they suspect the pasture belongs to that same farm upstate where they tell little boys their pets wound up."

"I thought that was against U.S. law."

"There's dogs in Pakistan."

212

The birch bark–clad rockers still lined the long front porch, looking as if they had never rocked since the day they left the factory. The floorboards creaked under his feet, a lonely sound, as if the ailing mistress of the house had already deserted it. Despite the evidence of constant maintenance, the house and the property it stood on reminded him of the generic ghost town in almost every western he'd ever seen; he half-expected to see tumbleweeds blowing across the sodded lawn and a gila monster sunning itself on the porch steps. The place was as haunted by its past as Hollywood itself.

His hand started toward the doorbell; but the thought of those chimes playing the chirrupy lead-in to *Red Montana's Frontier Theater* depressed him even more than his mission. He rapped on the screen door, its frame a scrollwork depicting a cowgirl playing a guitar and a cowboy spinning a lasso.

"You!"

Mrs. Chambers, whose fading streak of green hair still matched the color of her pantsuit, began to slam the paneled mahogany door. This time the visitor hadn't bothered to open the screen in order to block the movement. He merely held up the videotape Teddie Goodman had given him. It was labeled SAN GABRIEL STORAGE, and the date had been written in black marker. The door stopped moving as if it had sprouted roots.

"Since when do the duties of a nurse include breaking and entering?" he asked.

Her mouth moved several times before anything came out. He held up his free hand, stopping her. "There'll be time enough to tell your story in court. Right now I want to see your patient."

"In — court?" Her face lost several shades of color, restoring brightness to the verdant patch in her hair by contrast.

"It was your sore luck San Gabriel's security didn't cut costs by using black-and-white cameras. Next time you plan a felony, you might want to wear a hat."

"Sir, I've never —"

"I'm sure you didn't. The judge might go easy on you as a first offender.

"On the other hand," he added before she could respond, "Miss Day may provide information that would make me reconsider turning you in."

"Are you a policeman?" She looked doubtfully at his working uniform of windbreaker, T-shirt, and jeans.

On a sudden inspiration he produced one of his business cards, which read:

He held his thumb over the word film.

She nodded then, her chin wobbling, and stepped aside from the door. Sliding the videotape into his slash pocket, he followed her through a cavernous great room over-hung by a massive chandelier made from elks' antlers, past sofas and overstuffed chairs covered in mottled cowhide, a cavalry guidon tacked to a wall, chewed by bullets or moths, glass cases containing more of Red Montana and Dixie Day's career memorabilia, and through a sliding door into a bright sunroom walled in with glass on three sides.

Here sat an old woman in a wheelchair, her knees covered by an Indian blanket. A glass-topped rattan table supported a forest of prescription containers and brown glass medicine bottles, which had contributed to the sweetish smell of a hospital room.

"I've been expecting you," said Dixie Day, after her visitor had introduced himself. "I'll ring for you if I need you, Netta."

The door slid shut behind the nurse, and Valentino accepted his hostess's invitation to sit in a painted wicker chair facing her.

She was looking at him curiously. "My

mother had her picture taken with the original Valentino in the Cocoanut Grove when she was eighteen. You favor him."

"So I'm told. Thank you for seeing me, Miss Day. Or do you prefer Mrs. Montana?"

"Miss Day will do." The reply had a harsh edge.

Nearing eighty, the retired actress was still a beautiful woman despite the unmistakable signs of her illness. She had strong bone structure, and skillful makeup disguised most of the ravages of cancer. The turban she wore to cover the hair loss caused by radiation and chemo treatments lent her an exotic air, but he could still see in her that well-scrubbed, all-American quality that had won the simple hearts of postwar audiences. The Wild West Show glitter she'd worn in public was conspicuously absent from her present costume of blouse, slacks, and open-toed shoes, with a blue silk scarf wound around her throat; rapid weight loss would have made the skin sag.

"How is Dick Junior?" she asked. "All grown up and then some, I suppose. His father certainly kept him busy around the set."

He'd been puzzled when she'd said she was expecting him; now he knew Richard Hennessey, Jr., son of the cameraman who'd

216

shot Dixie's stag film, had called her. It didn't take too much thinking to figure out how the man had put two and two together, despite Valentino's discretion. It was quite likely that the woman whose company he now shared was the only surviving actress who had moonlighted for the elder Hennessey. The proprietor of Candy Box Pictures had not struck him as a dullard, nor as the type of man who wouldn't call and prepare her for an ordeal.

Valentino decided to spare her the extra unpleasantness of suspense. "I know who stole the film from the storage place," he said, patting the videotape in his pocket. "Or rather, who smuggled *Johnny Tremain* into it. I nearly abandoned the investigation when I figured that out. It was an act of expiation; a way of compensating Dick Junior for the theft.

"The blue movie was removed years ago. If there was any electronic security system in place then, the evidence would have been destroyed or taped over long since; most likely there wasn't any, or the burglary would have been reported, and Dick Junior would have told me. I believe him to be innocent, and his father committed suicide many years before the blackmailing began."

She watched him with a twinkle in her

eyes, still deep blue after all these years and despite the pain he detected behind them.

"Goodness, you *are* a detective. Whom do you suspect?"

He returned her gaze, hoping she wouldn't force him to say it. But there was nothing like mercy in those clear, clear eyes. She didn't seem not to possess it so much as to have moved past such considerations. He pushed on.

"I suspected your nurse when I recognized her on the surveillance tape; but I knew nothing about her, and having gotten to know your husband, I thought of someone who'd feel no guilt for exploiting a man so arrogant and mean because she had to put up with him every day for sixty years. That's you, Mrs. Monta— I mean Miss Day. You bled your husband for hush money before, and you're bleeding him again now, using the film you acted in as bait."

She laughed; and despite her age he heard the bell-shaped tones of her singing voice. "You're off the track, young man."

"I knew you'd deny it. I could threaten to turn Mrs. Chambers in to the police, where you know she'll confess eventually that she broke into that storage shelter at your request. Somehow, though, I think you won't put her through that. She must be very loyal to you to do what she did."

"You don't understand. I'm not protesting innocence. Yes, I've been blackmailing Red, or trying to."

"But you can't need money!" He stopped himself before saying, *especially not now.*

There was now no sign of amusement on the famous face. "Ironic, isn't it? When not so many years ago, money would have been the answer to everything.

"No," she continued, "I had nothing to do with how that film was removed from storage; but I have it, and I intend to use it against that rattlesnake I married until I draw my last breath."

22

"Not for the money," Dixie Day said. "He never really cared about that except as a tool to build a monument to the grand and glorious miracle that is Red Montana. Whether he comes through this time or not, I intend to use those reels to rip it off its pedestal and serve him the way tyrants were meant to be served."

"If you hate him that much, why didn't you divorce?"

"To protect my career, at first. We were a package deal, remember? When that no longer mattered, it wasn't enough just to slap him with a big settlement or alimony payments. I had to sting him where he was most vulnerable; his precious image." She paused; to gather strength, Valentino thought. "Mind you, there was a time when money *was* an issue. Did Red show you his treasure hoard in the museum basement?"

"Yes."

"I suppose he told you Joel McCrea presented him with William S. Hart's fancy revolver on his deathbed."

"Well, he didn't say *deathbed.*"

"Credit him for that, at least; most of his fantasies are too pat to be believed. He bought the gun at McCrea's estate auction. We were stuck at the time — Red went deep in debt buying up all his old films, and they'd yet to show a profit from television. My brother Brian was blind. I found a specialist who could restore his sight, but his fee was high and our insurance wouldn't cover the procedure."

She spread her hands, naked of the dazzling turquoise rings she used to wear in public; they shook a little. "You can die from lack of hope. Brian did, within a year. It wasn't until months later, when I read a feature in *Variety,* I found out Red had spent almost the exact amount the surgeon would have charged on that damn pistol!" Patches of angry color showed beneath her makeup. "You can't have failed to miss, Mr. Valentino, that my husband's world revolves around him."

"What did you mean when you said I'm off the track?"

"It's true I asked Netta to place that film in the storage facility. I'd have done it myself if I were up to it, and I'd be very upset to learn she were to suffer because of it; yes?"

Something about her, the iron core hidden inside that diseased frame, moved him to nod in assent. Come what may, Netta Chambers wouldn't be implicated in whatever came to pass.

"We've gotten close," Dixie Day said, "as you might expect from the relationship between a dedicated caregiver and a patient who's — well, patient. She went into the profession partially to atone for her spotted adolescence; since you've seen the security video, you no doubt noticed she's no amateur when it comes to picking locks."

"I wondered about that. They don't teach it in nursing school."

"They do, however, stress discretion. We shared confidences. A little larceny in the past must seem drab compared to complicity in extortion. It gained me some sympathy and Netta's cooperation; particularly having witnessed Red's true personality at close range."

"Complicity? You mean you had an accomplice before?"

"I was a victim. He came to see me while Red was in L.A., supervising the construction of the museum. He brought a print of the film with him. He offered to show it to me in our screening room, but I said that wouldn't be necessary. I knew what was on it. You saw some of the frame enlargements. I had a good body, don't you think?" She looked at him unblinkingly.

He had no idea what response she expected, so he went with the one that came to him.

"You were a beautiful woman."

"I was, wasn't I? It isn't really vanity when you can't claim credit for it: genes, Hollywood magic. You go with what God and Howard Hughes gave you."

"Who was he?"

"The blackmailer? Nobody, in the scheme of things. One of Dick Junior's temps; I doubt he'll remember him. Apparently, Dick sent him to the storage facility to reclaim a light stand or something, to replace one that had fizzled out; like his father's, that outfit gets along on whatever it can scrounge. The man stumbled upon the reels, knew enough about the industry to see the opportunity, and took advantage of it. Anyway, that's as much as he told me, to establish his credentials.

"The poor fellow. Do you know what he was asking for the film? Ten thousand dollars. I told him he could get ten times that

223

from Red. He said he preferred dealing with me."

"Did you pay him?"

"With what? I don't have any money. The museum, this ranch, all the bank accounts and investment portfolios — even my clothing line — are in Red's name. I haven't had control of a cent since we married. I have to ask him for money to visit the beauty parlor." She leaned forward, taking his wrist in an iron grip he'd hardly expected from a woman in her condition. "My husband is a small, stingy man, Mr. Valentino. And that's not even his worst quality."

Valentino said nothing. He felt he was on the verge of learning something he'd just as soon never know.

"Red has a violent temper," she said, releasing her grasp; circulation flooded back into his fingers. "Before my illness, all our friends thought I suffered from migraine. That's what Red told them when they visited and I was upstairs waiting for my bruises to heal. In 1960 he threw me down a flight of stairs and told the press I broke my leg while exercising Cocoa, my mare. I won't go into every incident. It galls him to pay the servants as much as he must to keep them from selling the real story to the tabloids. He's cheap, into the bargain; don't you find that funny?"

"No."

She acknowledged his veracity with a nod; and, he thought, a wisp of gratitude. "I suppose not. But it was enough to make me want to swap his meanness for some little act of apology. I had a walk-on in *The Great Locomotive Chase,* a Disney film; did you know that?"

He was completely thrown. "In what scene?"

"Trust a film buff to ask that question. It was a favor to an assistant director, after someone bailed out on him in the last minute. He couldn't admit his mistake to Walt, so he asked me what I wanted. I asked for a print of *Johnny Tremain;* my nephew was a big Revolutionary War fan. Well, he died in Vietnam. I'd read somewhere that the film was endangered, so I asked Netta to substitute it for what Dick Junior had lost."

She moved a shoulder, unconsciously exhibiting its boniness under the padded blouse. "Not much, I guess, in the way of justifying my existence; but it's how I've survived all these years."

"If you'd left him, you could have lived instead of just survived."

She directed her gaze outside the glass,

across the green expanse of the Circle M Ranch.

"Weakness," she said. "Pride. Red Montana and Dixie Day is one of the great love stories of Hollywood. Who was I to blow apart the fairy tale? The old studio system made us slaves to our public images. By the time I finally stopped caring, it was too late. You get used to living in hell. That doesn't mean you stop hating the devil."

"So when you didn't pay the man, he went to Red."

She smiled; the dazzling display of teeth possible only in Hollywood she'd showed the world.

"It was my suggestion! I even helped him work out the details. The only thing my husband has is the pure white image of Red Montana and Dixie Day. It's an icon. He's built his fortune on it; it's his ticket to immortality. I knew if the scheme succeeded I'd never hear a word of it from Red. I was right.

"He offered to split the money with me," she went on, "the little twerp. I didn't want it; but I did ask him for one thing."

Valentino sat back, feeling the heat of Southern California on his back; for some reason on that smog-free day, it made his skin crawl.

"A print of the stag film."

23

She smiled another Dixie smile, straight off the Miracle Bread package ("A sandwich as pure and bright as the King and Queen of the West"). Had the brand still existed, her listener would have fed his last loaf to the birds that congregated behind The Oracle; they at least would have appreciated it.

"I'd planned to release the film to an exhibitor when Red died, so he couldn't stop me," she said. "He's devious; a lot of people owe him favors, and he never forgets anything he did for anyone. But fate forced my hand." A sudden spasm distorted her expression, but she seemed to shake it off by sheer force of will. The blue eyes were brilliant in the ravaged face beneath the mask. "In a way I'm glad. Now I get to watch him suffer."

"You sent him the frame enlargements."

"A very old friend of mine made them in the film laboratory at Sony. It shocked him;

but I've passed beyond caring what people think of me. I felt the need to torment Red."

"I'm still not clear on how you got *Johnny Tremain*. Disney doesn't hand out prints, even to celebrities."

"Serendipity. Don't bother looking for my cameo in *Locomotive;* it never made it off the cutting-room floor, thanks to Red's influence. He couldn't stand the idea of any success of mine that didn't include him. Fess Parker pulled some strings to obtain *Tremain* for me. It was a quid pro quo, because I got him a walk-on in *Frontier Fandango,* and he felt bad that I didn't make the cut. I hadn't the heart to tell him I didn't know what to do with the thing. I'm glad he didn't live to see what I decided. He'd understand my wanting to make up for Dick Junior's loss, but he was an honorable man and would have felt guilty for his part in my little act of vengeance. Walt Disney never knew just how good a decision he made in casting Fess as Davy Crockett.

"Just knowing that stag film still exists will drive Red crazy until I'm gone. Then, when he can no longer hurt me, my friend at Sony will strike off additional prints and send them to every sleazy theater and cable station in Southern California. I made him promise to do it. Let Red try to exploit *that* for his own glory the way he did my terminal cancer. The whole world thinks he's a saint because of the Dixie Day Fund."

She sat back then, seeming to deflate inside her skin. The interview had exhausted her fully as much as the treatments she was no longer taking.

"This is the only thing I've had since our wedding that was truly mine."

A cloud — or more likely a scud of poisonous auto exhaust — had obscured the sun. Now it slid away, bathing the glass room in a deceptive ray of cheer. It made Valentino shudder as if a storm front had suddenly appeared.

Dixie Day balled her fists on the arm of her wheelchair. Beneath the clever cosmetics her face was a naked skull.

"Think of it, Mr. Valentino," she said, in a voice drained of all life force. "However long he outlives me, Red Montana will bear the stigma of the has-been cowboy hero who married Jezebel.

"And when he's gone, the world will be only too relieved to forget us both."

That sun-filled room in the Hollywood Hills had grown suffocating. He wanted to be anywhere else.

His hostess misinterpreted the source of his discomfort. "I'm sorry. Whatever he promised you, I assure you he won't honor it when he hears the truth. You'd be better off telling him you failed to identify his blackmailer. Is there something I can do to make it up to you? I'd offer to autograph a picture, but I don't think it will be worth much for long."

He thanked her for her time and staggered back out into the house proper, where Netta Chambers stood, hands folded in front of her and a look of absolute despair on her face.

He wanted to put a reassuring hand on her arm, but he sensed she'd flinch as if he'd raised it in anger. Instead he held out the surveillance tape. The earth revolved a bit on its axis before she took it in a hand that shook like the last leaf of autumn.

Pulling away from the turnaround in front of the porch, Valentino thought of *Sixgun Sonata,* that monument to chivalry and innocence, as thin as the celluloid it was made of. He didn't think he could watch it, or any Montana-Day picture, without seeing a bloated egomaniac and his battered, bitter wife.

He didn't breathe easily again until he'd

descended into the smog and smut of Los
Angeles.

24

The Oracle stood proud, its façade of polished stone belying the decay inside, retreating at glacial pace before the ongoing efforts to restore it to its Roaring Twenties glory. He'd sought comfort in the progress that had been made, but the contrast between work done and work still to be done only reminded him of the hatred and physical corruption hidden beneath Dixie Day's powder and paint.

Victor Stavros Senior did nothing to dispel Valentino's mood. He found the burly old Greek sitting on a crate filled with ceramic tile, weeping over a decrepit length of mahogany, which he'd removed from the filigree in the littered lobby. Around him, indifferent-seeming laborers pounded holes with sledges in the plasterwork, exposing frayed wires, ripped up hardwood floorboards with crowbars, and seemed in general to be inflicting more damage upon an already-suffering structure than restoring it. Valentino thought of firefighters swinging axes into the unburned walls of a building in flame.

"I know this work," Stavros said upon lifting his face to his employer's. "It could only have been done by a Florentine. Shall I die here?"

"Are you ill?" Valentino was alarmed; his mind this day was much on death.

"Sadly, I'm told I have no reason not to expect to observe my hundredth birthday. Thirty more years in this country seems to me like a sentence of imprisonment for life.

"Don't think me an ungrateful foreigner," he said, with a flush of shame. "This country has been good to my family. My son would never have found the opportunities he's had if we'd never come here. But the sun of California — when it shines — lacks the glow of Greece. It has shone on a thousand years of gods and poets, and the quality of its glow is like old copper, warmer than any hearth. The bones of my ancestors blaze there perpetually, bringing heat without consuming. The thought that I shall not be allowed to live out the rest of my days in its loving embrace, and be consigned to the earth of my grandfather and his grandfather's grandfather —" He trailed off, bereft of language to express an emotion Valentino felt as vividly as if he shared it; something he knew he could never do in equal measure.

"You're a poet yourself," he said, "and you don't exaggerate. I recovered a complete print of *Never on Sunday* in —"

"America is a good place, a noble place," Stavros said, unaware Valentino had spoken at all. "How can it be that a country so good and noble should snatch my son up by the only roots he's known and leave me, whose roots are in the land of my birth, to languish here?"

"I wish I could answer that." And he wished he could come up with a better response. As with Dixie Day, he felt the depth of his inability to touch the arm of one so afflicted. His respect for the man kept him from carrying out the action.

Stavros shook himself like an old bull throwing off a cloud of pesky flies, and rose to his full height. He was a big man, broad-shouldered and heavily muscled, every bit the kind of man Red Montana had seemed in feature after feature; and in his case genuine. A thick forearm swept the tears from the old man's eyes.

"The damage is not so great as I'd feared," he said. "Some of the original work can be saved. I can treat what's good, piece in what's needed, and finish the rest in less time than I thought. I promise you you will not be disappointed."

"I know that." *I wish I could promise you the same;* but he left that unuttered.

Fanta answered Kyle Broadhead's door, barefoot in a blue caftan that accentuated her height. She managed to look fresh despite long hours cramming for the Bar. Although the difference in their ages wasn't great, Valentino sometimes felt ancient in the presence of her feline grace and vast stores of energy; how a Jurassic creature like Broadhead kept up with her must have been the secret of how he'd survived his incarceration in a Yugoslavian dungeon. Her expression upon recognizing the visitor confirmed his suspicion that he looked as worn out as he felt.

Broadhead greeted him without rising from his old green recliner in the living room. Almost everything else about the place had changed since Valentino had roomed with him after being turned out of The Oracle by a corrupt building inspector: The dusty old rug had been replaced by something bright and contemporary, the gloomy pictures on the walls had ceded their territory to crisp black-and-white photographs taken by Fanta herself during a hiking trip across Europe, and some gloppy knickknacks left over from the professor's first marriage had been stored away and some sleek vases and stainless steel sculptures put up in their place. The tacky chair seemed to have survived only because its owner refused to get up from it long enough for the trash collectors to swoop in.

How long he'd be able to hold out against his fiancée's cheerful persistence was one for the office pool.

His host sat with his argyle-clad feet propped up and a tall glass of clear liquid at his elbow. Following the path of Valentino's glance, he scooped the glass off the end table and rattled the ice cubes.

"Mineral water. Flaming Youth there informs me it's too early in the day for gin-and-tonic. I can't convince her the sun set on the British Empire two and a half hours ago."

"You're lucky I don't cite Honolulu time when the cocktail hour does come around. Sit down, Val. What can I bring you?"

"Nothing, thanks."

Broadhead's rumpled face registered understanding. "My dear, pour our friend something stiff. If you'll look in my shirt drawer, you'll find a bottle of Polish vodka I smuggled through customs. I was saving it for the wedding night; but I know an emergency when I see one."

She glided out, to return a moment later carrying a tall glass bottle with Cyrillic lettering on the label. "Wait a minute," she said. "You haven't been to Poland since we became engaged."

"I didn't say *which* wedding night I had in mind originally. Your dear departed predecessor went teetotal on me during the courtship."

"My God, this is older than I am!"

Valentino, seated opposite Broadhead on a sofa with lines as clean as Fanta's, shook his head. "You'd be wasting it on me. It must be worth a fortune."

"Don't be ridiculous. It's rude to let a guest drink alone." He looked at Fanta. "It's even later in Moscow."

"You're right," she said, and carried the bottle into the kitchen.

Broadhead shook his head. "I can never anticipate her reaction to anything I say. Sometimes I think she'll bite my head off, and she laughs. Other times — tell me, is it youth or gender?"

"Kyle, she's as alien to me as she is to you.

I just know you're a lucky man."

She returned, carrying two glasses with ice cubes floating in clear liquid, handed one to Valentino, and folded herself into the other end of the sofa, holding the other. Sheepishly, Broadhead withdrew the hand he'd held out for the drink and picked up his mineral water.

"She's determined to celebrate my centennial. From what I've seen of that generation, I'm not sure I'm so lucky after all."

"Here's to crime." She lifted her glass.

Broadhead, eagle-eyed scholar that he was, saw that Valentino had barely touched his glass to his lips; the gimlet eyes in the sagging face said it all. He set down his glass. "Dear girl, I suddenly realize I'm famished. I'm certain our guest is as well. Would I be violating every principle of sexual equality if I asked you to fix us an omelet?"

"You know you would," she said. "Whites only, of course?"

"But of course."

Her own eyes, no less gimlet, shifted toward their guest; plainly, she saw through the maneuver; her absence was necessary. "Are you hungry?"

"Bless you, but I've never had less of an appetite."

She tapped her fingers on the arm of the sofa, sipped a gram from her glass, set it down — plainly leaving it accessible — and catapulted herself onto her feet. "Be back in a jiffy."

The two men sat in silence while something sizzled in the kitchen. At length, Broadhead rose, picked up Fanta's glass, and off-loaded half its alcoholic contents into his glass. He stirred it with a finger, tasted it, and threw himself back into his chair, swirling the contents. A sip, eyes closed in rapture, then:

"Not crime in all its forms, certainly. You and I and that angel in the kitchen, who just between us can't cook an omelet fit for a dog, have abetted in more than our share."

"Obstruction of justice, anyway." Valentino dredged up a weak smile.

"Purely a matter of observation, and open to interpretation. Blackmail's cut-and-dried; odious beyond even our flexible morals. Something tells me your investigation of same went south precipitously."

Valentino leaned forward, dangling his hands between his knees, and lowered his voice to a murmur. "You can't even share this with Fanta."

"But of course. I've racked my brains for some dread secret to keep from her. The absence of truth is the foundation of a great marriage."

"Kyle, please for once put aside the professional cynicism and open your ears."

Broadhead lifted his glass, but left it short of his lips. He returned it to the table, sat back, and folded his hands across his middle. "I lend them only, as advised by the Bard." The tone of his voice undermined the burlesque intended. Somewhere under those layers of academic crust beat a sensitive heart.

Valentino told it all then, including all the parts he'd left out earlier. Broadhead, the professional heretic, was visibly moved by Dixie Day's confession. He listened to Fanta's unnecessary labors in the kitchen — no egg entrée had ever consumed so much time — and touched the corner of his mouth.

"You have no place in this affair," he said. "It's between a man and his wife; or more precisely the mating of arachnids, one of whom devours the other. It's for you to decide if *Sixgun Sonata* is worth the sale of your soul."

Valentino sprang to his feet, balling his fists at his sides. He wanted to strike out at something: Who? Red Montana, hero of his youth, villain of his reawakening? Dixie Day, the bitter and revengeful queen of all that was pure? Slap O'Reilly, the real victim of the affair? The lowly opportunist at Candy Box Pictures who'd stumbled upon the key to his prosperity in two reels of grainy celluloid?

"I don't want the damn thing! It would only remind me of how phony this whole business is."

Kyle Broadhead, for the first time in his friend's memory, softened his expression. Valentino would sooner have expected it from the heads on Easter Island. Broadhead took a deep draught from his glass and set it down.

"*What*'s phony? The world we labor to preserve or the one that exists outside the stuttering lights on the marquee? As corrupt as Hollywood is, as nepotistic and sexist and bigoted and political and narcissistic, all it's ever sought to do is fulfill the dreams of those who lay down their hard-earned money to escape from their daily struggles, the will to survive; that's where the money is. Who cares if Red Montana's the real man in the black hat? Mallory gave us the Holy Grail, and he did time for rape. Ned Buntline sold us Buffalo Bill, and Buntline shot a man over the affections of the man's wife. Maybe it's the evil men who are best qualified to define the line between good and bad.

"Whatever you hear, the world's divided evenly between the one and the other. All you have to do is look at a thing long enough to see the difference. That's what the western has taught us; what Red Montana espoused, whether or not he believed in it when the director yelled 'Cut.' He couldn't lie without departing from the script."

Valentino drummed his fingers on the arm of the sofa, lifted his glass, took a long draught. The Polish vodka burned going down and lit a fire on the floor of his stomach; and likely heartburn in his future.

"Do you really believe it's as simple as that? Black and white, nothing in between?"

"Emphatically I do. I grew up on *Stagecoach* and *My Darling Clementine.*" Broadhead drank, swallowed. "But then, most of those cowpokes the hacks wrote about were half-blind on red-eye."

Fanta came back in empty-handed, frowned at her half-empty glass, shrugged, and sat. "Burned the eggs. I guess they're fit for a dog now. Heard you," she said, when both men stared. "Heard everything."

"Another quality of her tender years," her

fiancé told their guest. "I should have warned you."

25

"What do I tell Montana?"

"Nothing."

Broadhead and Fanta glanced at each other and laughed. They'd answered the question simultaneously.

"I don't know if I can do that," Valentino said. "He's in the way of being my client. I owe him some loyalty."

"Val." The young woman leaned forward, set her drink on the glass coffee table, and remained in that position, hands clasped between her knees. "If I've learned anything studying the law, it's when to keep your client in the dark. You know that old saw about making sausages."

"This is worse."

"It isn't. Trust me on that." Broadhead toyed with his glass. "I wasn't born with a Ph.D. Why do you think I never order the wurst plate in The Brass Gimbal?"

"You said it made you gassy," Fanta said.

"We didn't know each other so well then. A dyspeptic educator seemed more respectable than a meat-monger."

"Kyle wasn't born with a degree, and Dixie wasn't born bitter," she said. "She's what Red made her. He's the ogre, not the victim. Let her have this one victory before she dies. Remember, if it weren't for her you wouldn't have *Johnny Tremain.*"

"What happens to *Sixgun Sonata*?"

"You said you didn't want it."

"I don't. But letting him destroy it goes against everything I've worked for since I left college."

Broadhead had fallen silent. Sensing that muscular brain in action, Valentino looked at him and waited.

"What makes you think he'll destroy it?"

"He said he would."

"And you believed him?"

"You weren't there when he said he would."

"He's an actor and a fraud," Fanta said. "The man's whole life is a lie. The only thing he ever destroyed is his wife. He built that monstrous museum because he couldn't bring himself to get rid of anything. He even let his brother-in-law die so he could add another piece of crap to the pile. Call his bluff. If you tell him anything, tell

246

him the trail's cold and you've got too much responsibility to the university to waste any more time on it. I still vote for ducking him altogether. You're so honest he might see right through you."

"What if he isn't bluffing?"

"Think of it this way: Lose one film, gain another. I've never seen *Tremain,* but I'm betting it's worth more than Red Montana's whole filmography."

The telephone rang. She rose to answer it, said, "Yes, okay," and hung up. "I'm wanted at the office, damn it. Another paralegal took sick and had to go home."

"She's working part-time at Preston and Preston," Broadhead told Valentino. "They're taking no chances of her going to work for any other firm once she's bona fide. I'm sorry, my dear. I look forward to our quiet time."

"You're not sorry at all, you old soak. Finish this for me." She handed Broadhead her drink and left the room, returning moments later in heels and a gray silk suit and carrying a briefcase. The kitten of leisure had been replaced by a smart-looking young professional woman. She leaned down to kiss her bridegroom-to-be good-bye and went out, pausing to lay a hand briefly on Valentino's shoulder.

When the door closed behind her he said, "I have some good news. Sir Frederick Munn can make your stag party."

"Oh, him." The professor drank. "He was a resounding bore in Christ Church College and now he's a crashing one in an interesting job, running interference between the Foreign Secretary and the U.S. State Department. I think the Prime Minister selected him for the position because it meant he'd spend half the year three thousand miles away."

His guest groaned inwardly. "If you feel that way, why was he even on your list?"

"Vanity. Despite my pose of venerability, I didn't want you thinking I'm so ancient I'd buried all my friends. I suppose I'll have to put him up here. In addition to being tiresome, he's as cheap as Uncle Scrooge."

"If he's so dull, how'd you ever talk him into setting off a plumber's rocket in the faculty washroom?"

"Is he claiming credit for that now? In addition to being tiresome, he's now a plagiarist. He'd never have been knighted if the Queen knew he's dull as paint."

"Is that why you never told me you went to Oxford? You were embarrassed by your juvenile prank?"

"Certainly not. It's the only distinguishing

thing about my time there. Would you admire me as much if you knew I was a dropout?"

"No, but I'm beginning to admire you less right now." Valentino rose. "I'm handing in my notice. Find yourself another best man."

Broadhead stopped with the glass halfway to his lips. "Seriously?"

"Of course not. The only other man who could take the job is a crashing bore and a plagiarist."

"Hey, hotshot!"

He was walking down the street toward his car. Now he stopped to look at Teddie Goodman seated behind the wheel of her flashy red convertible, looking no less conspicuous in a designer outfit better suited to a runway than a residential street in L.A.

He went over. "Have you been following me all over town?"

"*Some*one thinks he's more important than he is," she said. "When the old bat in your office told me you weren't in — as usual, she said — and you weren't at that broken-down popcorn palace of yours, I figured you'd be schmoozing with your dinosaur buddy, and here you are. Who's that dish who just left?"

"The dinosaur's fiancée. You've seen her before."

"Not for a while. She's all dressed up like a grown-up. Does he keep her out past her bedtime?"

"What do you want, Teddie?"

"How'd you make out on that storage company video?"

Now was a good time to lie. "It wasn't any help. I couldn't identify the burglar, and I can't spend any more time trying to acquire *Sixgun Sonata.*"

"You're backing out of our deal?"

"I haven't anything to deal. I'm going to have to owe you some favor that doesn't include that film."

"Not good enough." The engine rumbled to life. "I already told Mark about it. He's chomping at the bit; turns out he's been a western fan since *Bonanza* premiered. If you're giving up, I'll have to make an end run around you and bargain with Red Montana direct."

Before he could respond, she threw in the clutch and peeled away from the curb.

"Back so soon? I thought my animal magnetism worked only with my future intended."

Valentino had caught Broadhead topping off his glass from the bottle of Polish vodka;

250

but if he'd expected any sign of embarrassment, it would mean an imposter had taken his mentor's place.

"I just ran into Teddie Goodman."

"And then did you back over her and do it again?"

"Of course not."

"Then it's no good. Cockroaches are easier to kill."

"If she makes good on what she just threatened, she'll know what I know in half the time it took me and spill it, stealing Dixie Day's thunder and the only thing she has to cling to in her last days." He told him what had passed between them. "As Fanta said, her revenge is all Dixie has. He may have enough clout to silence the whole thing."

"Teddie never makes a threat she doesn't intend to make good on." Broadhead sat back and set down his drink untasted. "We have to find something her boss wants even more than *Sixgun Sonata.*"

"There's no time for that! She's got that go-devil wound up, headed straight to Montana. If he makes her the same deal he did with me, she won't dither around. Dixie will be her logical next step, whether he makes her promise to leave her alone or not."

"Calm down. We already have it, thanks to Dixie."

Valentino blinked. "Not *Johnny Tremain.* Teddie said Turkus isn't interested."

"That's where you come in. Your Mickey Rooney enthusiasm can swing him over where guile and chicanery would fail. He's a tiger in the boardroom, knows all the corporate tricks, but he has one weakness, which is the same as your strength in this particular case: He's a movie buff. You must go to him in person and persuade him that next to *Tremain, Citizen Kane* is *Heaven's Gate.*"

"I'll have to move fast."

"Better to move sure. Remember, as far as Montana knows, you're still on the case. It will take everything she's got in her arsenal to make him change horses. He's a conniver himself, after all.

"As she said, Val, Turkus has been a western fan since the premiere of *Bonanza.* Do you know when that was?"

"I'm a movie guy, not a TV one."

"Nineteen-fifty-nine. *Davy Crockett* ran on Disney in that same era. I'll lay odds Mark David Turkus wore a coonskin cap when he was knee-high to Nelson Rockefeller. Fess Parker, who is everyone's Davy, put *Tremain* in Dixie's hands while he was starring in *The Great Locomotive Chase.* Use that. If the Turk is the collector he's made out to be, he'll be interested in everything connected to his obsession, however peripheral."

"It's thin."

"Then lay it on thick. Offer him distribution rights, and make it a condition that he pull Teddie off *Sixgun Sonata.*"

"What reason will I give?"

"None. Do you think a shark like him confides his motives in any business arrangement?"

"But we don't have the rights; Disney has."

"You're forgetting you're friends with a successful lawyer whose firm also specializes in Contract Law."

"Evan Overholt? But how can I get him to do it? I'm strapped as it is. Even if he offered me a courtesy fee, it'd be way outside my budget."

Broadhead cocked his head. His friend had told him of the incident at the Argyle Hotel.

Valentino blinked, then felt himself flushing. "I'm *not* going to ask Harriet to agree we swing with Overholt and his wife; that much sympathy for Dixie I don't have."

"Oh, very well. But there's another favor

you can do him. Is he still having trouble getting Immigration to lay off deportation proceedings against his client?"

"I have no control over that."

"I didn't say you did. I asked a question."

"Yes. He said Spraddle, the official, won't even meet with Victor Stavros Junior. They're at an impasse."

"When does Freddie Munn get in?"

Valentino had forgotten all about him. "The bore?"

"I may have been unkind. I haven't so many friends left I can afford to judge them. He can help me brush up on my whist. As I recall, he was good at the game, to the point of suspicion; it put a touch of color on his gray exterior."

"He cheated?"

"I can't accuse without evidence; but at present I find the possibility encouraging."

"Sir Frederick didn't mention his travel plans."

"Ring him up again. Tell him the stag party's next week and he should fly here as soon as possible."

"Traditionally, the party takes place the night before the wedding."

"So we mess with tradition. I'm not enough of a Dixie fan to get married in one week for her sake. Tell him old Broadbottom wouldn't think of letting him stay anywhere else."

"But why?"

Broadhead picked up his glass and drank deeply from it. "You've seen enough gangster movies to know you never plan a crime over the wire."

26

Mark David Turkus' reputation as a nerd was as carefully calculated as his career. His barber cut his ginger-colored hair on orders to make it look as if he cut it himself, the bulge under his argyle sweater vest suggested the presence of a plastic pocket protector, and his collection of vintage scuffed tennis shoes was legendary. His office, which took up the entire penthouse floor of a skyscraper he owned in Century City, was carpeted in Astroturf, an NBA regulation-size basketball hoop hovered above a potato-chip-tin wastebasket overflowing with crumples of paper, and what Valentino was certain was an original four-sheet poster of Errol Flynn swashbuckling through *The Adventures of Robin Hood* decorated the wall behind his workstation without a frame, a six-figure item affixed with curls of Scotch tape like a Kiss poster in a dorm room occupied by an overage college freshman. No effort had been spared to convince underinformed visitors that he was some kind of penniless intern sitting in for the czar of a media empire with a staff numbering more than the entire population of Monaco. *Forbes* had just moved him up to the ninth richest man in the world.

The real object, of course, was to underscore those final two facts with an elaborate show of indifference.

On paper, the man owned nothing. Everything, from the towering building to his Tweetie Pie socks, was registered for tax purposes to Supernova International, the company he'd founded in his parents' garage thirty years earlier.

He heard out Valentino's pitch with his distressed Keds propped up on the Ping-Pong table he used for a desk, stirring only once, to polish the clear lenses of his tortoiseshell spectacles with a plain cotton handkerchief, then replace them astride his nose. While they were off, shiny patches of flesh like dress darts betrayed his most recent visit to a Beverly Hills plastic surgeon to pare years from his sixty-something face.

Valentino begrudged him neither his vanity nor his posturing. (To do so would be to avoid the company of most of the people he had to deal with in Hollywood.) The Turk was a ruthless competitor whose deep pockets had done the Film Preservation Department out of many a rediscovered treasure, but that was business. Valentino distrusted the tycoon for another reason: He'd offered the film archivist Teddie Goodman's job while she was in the hospital recovering from injuries sustained in the search for the original *Frankenstein* test reels. Compared to her employer, Teddie was a sentimental pushover.

"You make a good case," he said when his visitor paused; "and I do prefer working with UCLA rather than in competition, but I'm not much of a Disney fan. The studio's historical dramas are too squeaky-clean for my taste. Even Long John Silver looks like he showered daily with Ivory soap."

Valentino forbore explaining that *Treasure Island* wasn't historical. There were surprising gaps in the education of many a self-made man.

"That period of Technicolor did like to make its hues pop," he conceded. "If I can't appeal to your interest as a film buff, I can refer to the monetary angle."

"I doubt you can make that stick. Hollywood's shot hundreds of Civil War films, but only a handful about the American Revolution, and they've seldom made back the investment. The audience was force-fed Paul Revere and Bunker Hill to the point of nausea back in first grade. Maybe in another generation, now that the emphasis is shifting."

"There have been hits as well: *The Patriot* on the big screen, *John Adams* on TV."

Turkus uncorked his famous bashful grin. In early days he would have practiced it before a mirror as often as Arnold Schwarzenegger had pumped iron. "Those are isolated examples. I'd rather gamble on a trend than a hunch based on the exceptions."

"Warner Brothers is taking the plunge. They've taken an option on *Burr* for adaptation from the Gore Vidal estate."

"I hadn't heard that."

"It hasn't been announced yet. If the option runs out while they're still assembling the nuts and bolts and another studio hears Warner was interested, it might pull the project out from under them. As you can —"

He stopped, hoping he was pulling off an acceptable expression of self-loathing. "Please forget I said that. It's inside information."

If he expected his host to make any show of eagerness, he was disappointed. This alpha dog wagged his tail only in private.

"Well, if you've nothing more you want to say, I have a plane to catch. I'm attending a conference in Tokyo Friday."

You own the plane; it'll wait. Aloud, Valentino said, "Please don't tell anyone I said anything. I could lose my job."

Turkus made a noncommittal gesture with one freckled hand.

"An assistant professor of history I know told me about *Burr.* He's been approached by the studio to act as an uncredited consultant during filming. The head of the department thinks the movie business is beneath the dignity of the university. If he finds out, he might interfere with the man's chances for tenure."

"Then the man should turn down the job."

"It pays two thousand a week. He owes forty-seven thousand in student loans."

He watched Turkus' face for some sign that he suspected he was being sold a bill of goods, but there was none. What his professional instincts hadn't managed to smooth out, his cosmetic surgeon had.

"Still, it's a stab in the dark. These days, the studios go in together on big-budget productions so that if they flop, the loss is spread out. Any partnership between Supernova and the academic world would hardly be bulletproof. Forgive me for being blunt."

"Of course. It's no secret our board of regents would rather invest in the sports program than film preservation. But my friend learned something else while visiting the lot."

Again he fell silent. He heard Kyle Broadhead's voice: *I said lay it on thick. I didn't say use a trowel.*

For the first time, the wheeler-dealer showed a spark of impatience. Either that, or a scalpel-damaged nerve in one cheek had developed a twitch. "Tokyo, Mr. Valentino."

"Well, I've come this far." He leaned forward in his chair, a wood-laminate veteran of some boarded-up high school, and placed his own palms on the table. He'd avoided that before, knowing he'd leave wet patches on the green slate. Now they'd only add to the veracity of his tall tale. "These things will leak out, no matter how tightly they try to seal the lid. Tri-Star got wind of *Burr,* and is going ahead with plans to shoot a biopic about Ethan Allen."

"The furniture company?"

How could a man so ignorant amass billions? He forced himself not to show resentment. "Sir, *this* Ethan Allen commanded a force of irregulars during the battle of Ticonderoga in 1775. The working title of the film was taken from the name of his band: *The Green Mountain Boys.*"

"Yes, of course. I'd forgotten for a moment." Turkus took his feet off the table and sat up. "You're sure of this information?"

But he'd lied enough for one afternoon. "You know this town. It holds confidential information like a paper bag holds water."

"Suppose I say we have a deal: exclusive distribution rights to *Johnny Tremain* in revival theaters, DVD, and we split the proceeds equally. What makes you so sure you can obtain the rights? The shark in *Finding Nemo* was based on Disney's lawyers."

"Would I waste your time and mine if I didn't have a plan in mind?"

"Would you? Possibly. You're not as clever as Teddie. I'm glad now you didn't take me up on my offer when she was, um, unavailable."

"Speaking of Teddie," Valentino said, and delivered the rest of his terms.

27

"Pipe that, will you?" Broadhead said. "At school, his pink ties and yellow socks were the only bright things about him. Now that he's in the diplomatic service he looks as if he's seen every picture Ealing Studios ever made."

Waiting in Baggage Claim at LAX, Valentino and Broadhead watched Sir Frederick Munn descend the steep flight of stairs. A man of medium height, inclined toward stoutness, he wore a black bowler with the brim squared across his brow and a single-breasted suit to match under a Burberry trench coat. His tie was black also, as were his highly polished oxfords (what else?) and the tightly furled umbrella he carried opposite the leather dispatch case, appropriately dilapidated, in his other hand. His sandy moustaches were expertly trimmed and waxed at the tips. At sight of his old schoolmate he broke into a broad grin that showed a gap between his front teeth. For once, a picture the archivist had formed over the telephone had proven accurate. He was every American casting director's idea of the typical upper-class Englishman.

"Broadbottom, my dear old chum! What a jolly pleasure. How long has it been?" He wrung Broadhead's hand.

"Harry Breathwaite's funeral, six years ago. It seems much more recent." The professor shook circulation back into his fingers. "Munny, this is Valentino, my friend and colleague."

"A pleasure, Sir Frederick." He buried his hand deep in the visitor's palm to spare his own fingers.

"No titles, please. Freddie for now. You can call me Munny when we know each other a bit better."

He retrieved a brace of matched suitcases embossed with a crest from the carousel and Valentino carried them to his car. With them safely stored in the trunk (*boot?*), he slid behind the wheel. Broadhead sat beside him.

"You'll stay with me, of course," Broadhead said to the diplomat in the back seat.

"How very kind. You know, Val— it is Val, isn't it? Your Christian name?"

"Val it is," he said evasively. "No titles,

remember?"

"Kyle and I were roommates up at Oxford. I don't suppose he's told you of our adventures."

"I know about the plumber's rocket in the washroom."

"Har-har! Capital!" He spent half the next ten miles recounting the incident in detail. By the time he came to their suspension, he'd made an explosion at the world's most respected university seem as exciting as a lecture on soap manufacture. His old friend interrupted him just as he began to repeat the whole thing from the start.

"That was before we landed in Egypt with Caesar. How tight are you with the U.S. attorney general, Munny, old man?"

"Oh, we get on. He's a bally bad golfer, but I'm good enough to cock up a few shots and level the field."

"I'm glad to hear it. I've a favor to ask, and it involves the State Department and Immigration."

Both men were silent as Valentino turned into the driveway. Sir Frederick Munn's reflection in the rearview mirror had shed its bifurcated grin and the forehead under the bowler had developed more wrinkles.

"That's a tall order, Kyle. I don't know

265

that our relationship is solid enough for me to risk an international incident."

"Hardly that. If the thing ever comes to light it can be brushed off as just another bureaucratic blunder, and hardly a crucial one. Even the administration's fiercest enemy couldn't make over a Greek cabinet-maker into the head of Al-Qaeda."

"But what's your interest?"

Valentino told him as much as he could without giving away Dixie Day's secret. His closest friend was placing himself in the diplomat's debt in order to help Valentino keep his job, and in the bargain render a great service to an old man who wanted nothing more than to finish his life in his native land.

"I gather this all has to do with some motion picture. I think before I consider this extraordinary request I should have the privilege of knowing what it is."

Broadhead broke in before Valentino could say *"Johnny Tremain."*

"*Sixgun Sonata,* starring Red Montana and Dixie Day."

"Montana and Day are —" Valentino started to explain.

But he was interrupted again, this time by Munn, whose grin sprang back into life.

"A western! Oh, jolly good! Broadbottom

and I skipped class every time one of their features came to the village. Why on earth didn't you say so in the first place? It's a bloody well better reason to play a prank than our last one."

Evan and Laura Overholt were still registered at the Argyle. Valentino asked the desk clerk to ring up their room and ask them to meet him in the lobby. The handsome blond therapist and her redheaded lawyer husband alighted from the elevator twenty minutes later and they found a quiet corner furnished with deep leather chairs. The couple was dressed casually — for them — she in a silk blouse and pleated slacks, he in a fine-checked sportcoat and black jeans with a designer label.

Laura looked around. "Is Harriet with you?"

"I'm afraid not."

"Oh. I thought perhaps —"

Valentine managed not to blush. "I'm afraid not, but we were more flattered than offended. You know what she does for a living, and I've lived in this town longer than I lived in Indiana. Not much shocks us."

"Then — ?" Evan raised his eyebrows quizzically.

"The other day you said you weren't making much headway with Immigration. Is that still the case?"

"I'm afraid it is. Spraddle's your typical narrow-minded bureaucrat, nasty piece of work."

"Good. For me, I mean. I am sorry for your troubles."

Laura said, "Now you must come out with it before we burst."

"I know you specialize in Immigration issues," Valentino told Evan. "You said your firm also handles cases involving Contract Law."

"It does. I practiced it for a while, but I found the former more interesting and went back for retraining."

"Did you ever negotiate a deal with a major corporation?"

He smiled politely. "I suppose it depends on what you'd call major. Does Hilton Worldwide count?"

"It does. Are you familiar with *Johnny Tremain*?"

Evan's eyes rolled toward the coffered ceiling. "Directed by Robert Stevenson, starring Hal Stalmaster, Luana Patten, Jeff York, and Sebastian Cabot, released in 1957 by Walt Disney Productions." He laughed at the reaction. "I've been a history buff all my life. How do you think I got interested in westerns?"

"In that case I have good news and bad news. The bad news is the film's been considered lost for years. As far as materials, safety stock is superior to silver nitrate, but the colors fade with time. The bright shiny film you remember is gone. Or it was."

"Which brings us to the good news," Evan said. "You've found a copy in restorable condition."

"I haven't examined it in detail, but I believe so."

"How exciting, and romantic!" said Laura. "Where did you find it? I've heard of discoveries in Siberian landfills and sunken tankers."

"It was in a storage shelter in Pasadena."

"Oh." She sat back.

"I haven't screened it, but the colors in the frames I held up to the light are much more vivid than in other prints I've looked at the same way. Anyway, I was encouraged enough to have made an arrangement with Supernova International to join with UCLA in releasing it when it's ready. But Disney usually reserves everything for itself, and it has the money to finance the reconstruction and all the commercial arrangements, so we have nothing to offer it doesn't already have."

"You do need a lawyer. His job is to keep them from figuring that out."

"Naturally I don't begrudge the studio its wish to reap all the profits from its own property, but my loyalty is to my department and I think it should share the proceeds from a discovery I made in its employ. We need an attorney well-versed in Contract Law to pursue an agreement beneficial to all concerned."

"Doesn't the university have a legal staff?"

"Smith Oldfield is excellent, but his track record with Disney is dismal. It's gotten to the point where his past differences with their team is an obstacle." Which was true: Even the gentlemanly and ultraconservative New Englander had exhausted all his patience with the terriers in the studio's pit.

"Why not use Supernova's legal staff? They're a close match to Disney's."

Time for some more truth. "Too close, I'm afraid. They might get the idea they could swing the deal without us, and they'd be right."

Evan pursed his lips. "I'd have to brush up, and to meet with your people to know what you require and then climb into the ring with theirs."

"I need results by next week."

"Good God! Your board would never approve the fee I'd have to charge."

"Actually, that's one of the reasons I thought of you. I'm hoping you might consider adjusting it."

The lawyer looked at his wife, who returned his smile with a disbelieving shake of the head. He swung his gaze back to Valentino. "With all respect, we haven't known each other long enough to have become quite that close."

Laura Overholt's smile shifted subtly. "Dear, perhaps Val has something to propose other than friendship." She leaned forward and touched the visitor's knee.

This time he did blush.

"I'm still flattered," he said; and the hand was withdrawn with a frown. "But Harriet would never agree to that even if I were tempted." He looked at Evan. "Please don't take that the wrong way."

"Oh, I'm devastated. I've been told I resemble a young Brad Pitt." But he sounded irritated for the first time. Valentino suspected he *was* offended.

"What I have to propose is even racier than that."

Their expressions made his next question unnecessary, but he asked it anyway.

"Shall I go on?"

28

Valentino used Broadhead's influence to reserve the saloon at Universal for the bachelor party. He'd had a sign made reading THE BAR XO and hung it from the porch roof. Shockingly, all the chairs at the long table were filled. At the last minute, friends from the professor's past responded that they'd be delighted to wish him bon voyage on the sea of matrimony, whitecaps and all. They ranged from middle to old age, from fit to crumbling, and occupied (or were retired from) professions of every stamp, from inside and outside the entertainment community. One, a small gray man wearing a gray suit, gray necktie, gray shoes, and fringe of gray hair, spoke with a thick Eastern European accent. Valentino missed his name in the din of conversation, but from his speech and the heavy-duty cut of his ill-fitting coat and trousers, he suspected that the man had had something to do with the time the guest of honor had spent imprisoned in Yugoslavia. He and Broadhead closeted themselves in a corner for a good twenty minutes, all of it spent in earnest conversation, and all — so far as the eavesdropper could tell — in some Slavic dialect.

Sir Frederick Munn quickly became inebriated. His face was the bright red of an emergency flasher.

"He's earned a good toot," Broadhead said to his best man when the diplomat cleared a load of crystal glasses off one side of the table with the umbrella he seemed to have forgotten he still clutched under one arm. "He's pulled off the biggest switcheroo since *A Tale of Two Cities*."

"I just hope it doesn't come back to haunt him."

"The Good Old Boy Network will keep the spooks at bay. He's grandfathered in better than a tenured professor."

Every head turned when a woman entered the room. The spectacle was a sensation on two levels: A female had dared to crash a stag event, and an uncommonly tall and handsome mature one who'd attract attention anywhere she went. Her waves of beautifully coiffed white hair, tasteful wool dress that brought out the green in her eyes, and matching Gucci pumps and Prada bag suggested either a highly successful businesswoman or well-off widow; but her height was her most distinguishing feature. She stood at least six-foot-two in her modest heels.

Broadhead broke off his exchange with Valentino to approach the intruder. "Lucille?"

She answered him in a modulated contralto. "You can call me Lou. Don't worry, I won't stay. It's against all the rules, thank God and Dr. Habib. But I couldn't bring myself to steer clear when I heard about the affair. I hope we're friends. I'm still Lou Corelli, Glenn Ford's old gofer. Nothing's changed. Well, *one* thing." The newcomer's laughter was nervous.

"Don't be absurd. What good's a herd of stags without a doe to admire?" Broadhead turned to Valentino. "Did you forget to invite Lou?"

The archivist knew better than to correct him. "I don't know how I overlooked him — her!" he added quickly. "I'm terribly sorry."

"You've been under a strain." He patted the young man's shoulder. To Lucille: "I can't imagine anyone who's worked in this town giving you any trouble, but if they do, refer them to me."

Suddenly, the newcomer stooped and hugged Broadhead. She broke off in masculine fashion, smacking his back with both palms, and inclined her head in the direction of the big flat-screen TV mounted on one wall. "I think I'll check out the game, if it won't disrupt your celebration. The hormone shots haven't done anything to alter my choice of recreation."

"Be my guest."

"That was a wonderful display of friendship," Valentino said as the stately lady drifted off.

The professor shook his head, watching his friend's retreat. "What I can't understand is why they're always so tall."

They accompanied each other to the refreshment table, laid out with all the delicacies Southern California had to offer. Smearing caviar on a bagel, Broadhead asked which strip club Harriet was taking Fanta to for her wedding shower.

"Nothing so cliched. She's reserved a room at the bar where the police hang out."

"How inconducive to a good time."

"Not especially. She hired entertainment."

"Let me guess: Officer Wottahunk, complete with breakaway uniform."

"Actually, he comes in dressed in a striped

jersey and a little black mask, like the Ham Burglar."

It had been a busy week. On top of the last-minute arrangements for the party, Valentino had taken reports on Evan Overholt's successful negotiations with Disney to share the rights to *Johnny Tremain* three ways (in the corporation's favor, naturally; but there would be plenty of profits left over for Supernova and UCLA's Film Preservation Department) and from Sir Frederick Munn, who by promising certain concessions from the Court of King James had obtained the State Department's agreement to pressure Ernest Spraddle, the Immigration official assigned to Victor Stavros Junior's deportation proceedings, to accelerate the case. The intimidated official — who'd never met either Stavros — was relieved when the Greek waived his opposition, and upon reviewing the action, reported that Victor Stavros was no longer of concern to the government.

Said Munn, "We've these same slipshod fellows on our side of the pond. A Victor Stavros is required, and a Victor Stavros is delivered. If anyone is called upon to pay the piper, it will be that twit Spraddle. It would have happened eventually in any event."

"He's not alone," Valentino said. "I'm out a wood carver."

And so Stavros Senior prepared to return to his homeland at Washington's expense while Junior remained in the United States to apply for citizenship. This favor settled the question of Overholt's fee for his services (and cost Valentino two bruised ribs when the old man wrapped him in his powerful arms upon learning the news).

Fanta hadn't been pleased. "I know I'm not qualified yet, but it would have been nice to be asked to sit in with Overholt during the meetings with Disney."

Broadhead had shaken his head. "Munn's bulletproof, and Overholt's been in the trenches long enough to distance himself, but if the Immigration flap blows up, Spraddle's hide alone might not satisfy the piper. It's always the small fish that gets cut up into chum."

"How flattering." But she conceded the point.

Valentino knew there was more involved than just a harried minor official and careless paperwork; strings had been pulled, promises made on an international level, all off the record. But he was intelligent enough not to ask.

Harriet, who had been in on the conversation, said that as an employee of the Los Angeles Police Department she should report the whole business.

Broadhead said, "Why make a federal case out of it?"

Months later, Valentino paid the duty and COD to claim crates containing whole sections of beautifully wrought mahogany filigrees packed in bubble wrap. All that was required was a competent finish carpenter to assemble and install the sections. No bill for the work ever appeared.

At the time of the stag party, however, he was depressed. The day before, the media had reported that Dixie Day, the beloved leading lady of western musicals and long-time wife of singing cowboy star Red Montana, had died of uterine cancer. It wouldn't be long now before the blue movie Montana had tried so hard to suppress came to light.

"I know how to cheer you up," Broadhead said. "You were reluctant to book a film for this bacchanal, so I took the liberty of doing it myself." He inclined his head toward a middle-aged man in a flannel shirt and faded jeans, carrying a folding screen and a square case big enough to contain a projector, and introduced a member of the projectionists' union. When his mentor swept up the cloth hanging off the edge of the refreshment table to reveal a cardboard shipping carton with four film cans stacked neatly inside, Valentino's heart sank.

"How could you possibly think a stag film would cheer me up? Have you forgotten how this whole thing started?"

The other slid out one of the cans and held it up between his hands. The title was stenciled on the lid:

SIXGUN SONATA
Republic 52/124

Valentino sank onto a folding metal chair. "How — ?"

"It came to the department by special messenger this morning. I suppose Red thinks the threat's over now that Dixie's dead. We know differently; but his ignorance is our gain. It's in good screening condition, based on the first reel. I couldn't watch the others and not be late for my own bachelor party."

"The deal was the film in return for the blackmailer. I know Montana well enough to know he wouldn't change his mind."

"He would if he were offered the keynote speech at commencement and an honorary Ph.D."

Valentino stared.

"Chaves County, New Mexico, made him an honorary deputy sheriff two years ago," Broadhead went on. "They had their eye on persuading him to move his soccer team to Roswell; that alien thing is losing steam. Not to be outdone, the Texas Rangers swung him a make-believe commission in their ranks, complete with gold-plated badge: The Acapulco Piranhas could just as well be grounded in Amarillo, and they wouldn't even have to change their initials. Of course, L.A. wouldn't mind a shot at the World Cup. Do you think that prancing dandy would pass up the chance to be addressed as '*Dr.* Montana?' "

"But you don't have the authority to offer him a doctorate. The university has already arranged for the governor to speak at commencement."

"What does a cowboy star know of academic politics? For that matter, what do *you* know? It's why I'm head of the department, to run interference between zealots like you and the real world."

"I resent that; I think."

"Whatever, as Fanta's so fond of saying when I've scored a point. When I spoke to Montana on the phone this morning — not forgetting to offer my condolences on his tragic loss — I suggested that a gift of one of his rarer features to the university would guarantee front-page coverage across the country. It's a language he understands. He asked if we might be interested in his first film with Dixie — purely in tribute to his late wife. Offering *Sixgun Sonata* right out from under your deal; does *that* sound like the Red Montana you've come to know?"

"Kyle, you've made yourself a powerful enemy. Dixie made arrangements for the blue film to be released immediately upon her death. He'll already be mad as a hornet when he finds out you've tricked him."

"How long do you think his powerful admirers will stand by him once they've heard about his dear dead wife?"

"Kyle."

"I'm sorry. That was low. I withdraw the remark."

"Not that." The archivist pointed toward the flat-screen TV. His hand shook.

Although Lucille Corelli was watching it with the sound turned all the way down, Red Montana's figure filled the screen in an interruption of the broadcast, silently going through the frenetic paces of one of his old westerns. As all the room's occupants swung their attention that way, Broadhead's old friend reached up and turned up the volume just as the image dissolved to a talking head.

". . . hero of dozens of westerns, was found dead this morning in the curator's office in the Red Montana and Dixie Day Museum, which closed earlier this month. A spokesman for the museum said he shot himself accidentally while cleaning a revolver from his collection. Police, however, are investigating whether he might instead have committed suicide in grief over yesterday's passing of Dixie Day, his co-star and wife of many years. She was diagnosed . . ."

The talking head was replaced by one of Dixie's scenes in *Romance of the Range*.

The screen went black. Lucille had switched off the power.

"He was grieving, all right," Broadhead said. "Over his lost reputation. Whoever she trusted with that stag film must not have wasted any time telling him what to expect. Everyone will be watching her true motion-picture debut by the eleven o'clock report." Once again he placed a hand on Valentino's shoulder. "I'll send the projectionist home. I don't suppose anyone's interested now in watching a movie, particularly that one."

29

The game went strictly according to Hollywood Hoyle.

TMZ aired the first available footage of Dixie Day's smut film, heavily edited;

The Internet posted it in all its grainy original unabridged condition;

A breaking-news report reported that the gun that had killed Montana had been presented to him by Joel McCrea, "the late cowboy actor," who'd gotten it from William S. Hart "star of silent western films" ("Dixie might have orchestrated it herself," was Kyle Broadhead's comment);

The same celebrities who'd heaped praise on the "love story of the century" on *Entertainment Tonight* expressed shock and revulsion on *The Hollywood Insider;* some of them forgetting they'd attained fame with their own sex tapes;

Psychiatrists analyzed the Montana-Day mind-set (fists nearly flying between the

Freudian and the Jungian);

An anti-porno group held a rally in Springfield, Missouri, calling for the destruction of all their films;

The satellite and cable networks ran round-the-clock film retrospectives;

A national talk-show host welcomed an eastern movie critic who cited the fall from grace as further proof that the western was dead, and a spokesman for the National Cowboy and Western Heritage Museum who said zombies didn't rise from the grave as often as the western;

A TV reporter unearthed Sam "Slap" O'Reilly from the Motion Picture Country Home, dressed him in a yoke-shouldered sportcoat and milk-white Stetson borrowed from some studio wardrobe department, sat him in front of a garish poster of *Texas Two-Step,* and nodded in sympathy as Red Montana's beloved sidekick delivered a dry-eyed eulogy to his old screen partner (and a teary one to Dixie);

CBS, NBC, and ABC greenlighted TV movies, titled along the lines of *Red and Dixie: Behind the Guitar.* One by one, they ceased "pre-production." ("What's that?" Broadhead commented. "Meetings over frittatas?")

Christie's Auction House held a two-day

event selling off lots from the Montana-Day Estate. In a spirited contest, Mark David Turkus outbid Laura and Evan Overholt for the great stallion Tinderbox on his pedestal.

"*Now* will you tell me whether he had him stuffed?" asked Harriet, when the results were announced.

Valentino shook his head. "Just because Red went back on his word doesn't mean I will."

"He didn't deserve you as a fan."

And in a little while, as other sad ends and scandals sandwiched themselves between coming attractions and red-carpet events, all the vivid memories of the Sweethearts of the Range rode off into the sunset.

And when he's gone, the world will be only too relieved to forget us both.

But not Valentino.

"I grew up on Red Montana and Dixie Day," he said.

"As did I," said Broadhead.

"Thanks for clearing that up. You seem to want everyone to think your span is biblical."

"Even the pretense of immortality is an advantage when you're dealing with the administration."

"The little kid in me can't accept that when Montana talked so much about shooting straight he didn't mean it."

"Who says he didn't?"

"Montana, every time he opened his mouth off-screen."

"No one's that good an actor. Certainly not Red Montana. The camera never lies."

"Do you think he and Dixie ever loved each other?"

"What I think doesn't matter. Whatever happened when the film stopped rolling, only they could know. I do know that success is like dope. You can overdose on it, be poisoned by it. At some point, he forgot he was plain Lionel Phelps, but she never lost sight of Agnes Mulvaney. That's when they parted ways."

"So the Sweethearts of the Range are — ?"

"Still up there on the screen, ten feet high and ten feet wide. No lie could live on that scale."

The fallen idols remained on Teddie Goodman's mind as well. Turkus' queen barracuda never forgot a valuable property or a loss to a rival.

Valentino felt a distinct frisson of déjà vu when he opened his office door and saw her behind his desk, aimlessly swiveling right and left with her slender hands resting on the arms of his chair, her long legs curled beneath her. The crutches were no longer present; she was ready to swim unhindered and follow the scent of blood in the water. This time she wore a shimmering green shift of uncomfortably reptilian design. Her dagger-like nails (grown from scratch, not stuck on) matched the dress.

"So competing fair and square doesn't suit you after all," she said. "You had to trick Mark into calling me off *Sixgun Sonata*. And you so high and mighty on the subject of integrity."

She pronounced the word as if she'd just Googled it. He couldn't think how else she'd have discovered its definition.

"Couldn't risk it, Teddie. There was a time factor involved." He remained standing.

"There always is; which is why I don't mess with Boy Scout rules."

"I didn't like doing it."

"Which makes it okay, in your book." She showed perfect white teeth in her predatory Theda Bara smile. "Well, you'll get over that. The second time's always easier."

"There won't be a second time."

She was silent for a moment, the chair motionless. Then she got up all of a piece, like a serpent springing from a coil.

"That's just what *I* said," she said. "The first time."

■ ■ ■ ■

Kyle Broadhead, accompanied by Fanta, found Valentino and Harriet Johansen seated in the screening room of the UCLA Film Preservation Department, awaiting their first look at *Sixgun Sonata*. The same union projectionist the professor had hired for his party was doing the honors; trust the archivist to make good on his full fee. Broadhead had rescued an unopened bottle of champagne from the event, and brought it, along with four flutes. He filled them and handed them around. After toasting the upcoming nuptials in silence, the two couples settled in to watch the rest of the picture. Red Montana came galloping in aboard mighty Tinderbox to foil a stagecoach robbery, and shared a studio exterior with a luminous Dixie Day — her few minutes on-screen in a group of fellow unknowns gathered around a campfire. When, seemingly impromptu, her husky contralto came in on the third line of Red's serenade, the audience forgot all about cardboard trees and painted sky. It was the song the couple would perform in duet at the end of each episode of *Red Montana's Frontier Theater:* "Friendly camping on the

Owl-Hoot Trail, there's no place so good. . . ."

The four spectators joined in, each man twining his arm around his sweetheart.

CLOSING CREDITS

The entertainment world will never again witness a phenomenon like the western. To assume it's finished merely because it doesn't claim as large a part of the market as it once did is like a major corporation insisting it "lost" money because its profits weren't as big this year as last.

The subcategory of the western musical began shortly after movies learned to speak aloud. When a young John Wayne balked at repeating his role as "Singin' Sandy," warbling a ballad (dubbed by a professional singer) on his way to a gunfight, Republic Pictures signed Gene Autry to appear in *In Old Santa Fe*.

The obvious similarities between Red Montana and Autry — and between the Roy Rogers/Dale Evans team and Montana and Dixie Day — are entirely superficial. By all accounts, all three performers were as good in life as they were on-screen. The decades-long marriage of Rogers and Evans is one of the great love stories of Hollywood.

The following is a selected list of recommended titles in print and on celluloid. Even to limit it to merely the greatest would strain the budget of both publisher and reader. Please consider it a guide toward establishing your own roster of favorites.

Who we are, and who we like to think we are, say the same thing about us. Western culture is defined by the culture of the western. It's been estimated that westerns comprise ninety percent of all the films ever shot. However you feel about the historical roles of men, women, government, the army, the American Indian, and their fates, this much is true: If you don't like westerns, you don't like movies.

— *Loren D. Estleman*

BIBLIOGRAPHY

Bischoff, Peter, Krug, Christian, and Nocon, Peter, editors. *Studies in the Western
Volume VIII.* Muenster, Germany: The German Association for the Study of the Western, 2000.

With certain exceptions, foreign countries
appreciate American art forms more than
America, which often takes its treasures for
granted. This edition of the annual journal,
which like the others contains articles in
both German and English, contains a fine
cover essay by Andrea Grunert analyzing
the multiple layers of John Ford's *The Man
Who Shot Liberty Valance,* the movie (based
on Dorothy M. Johnson's novel) that gave
us the line: "When the legend becomes fact,
print the legend." This is a concise explana-
tion of the mechanism behind the frontier
myth.

Bischoff, Peter, Nocon, Peter, and Scholz,

Michael, editors. *Studies in the Western Volumes XIV & XV.* Muenster, Germany: The German Association for the Study of the Western, 2008.

As with every edition, this one contains a wealth of valuable material, but the late great western novelist Elmer Kelton's article, "Racial Relations in the Western," is particularly fine in its treatment of its theme regarding novels and film.

Cary, Diana Serra. *The Hollywood Posse: The Story of a Gallant Band of Horsemen Who Made Movie History.* Norman, Oklahoma: University of Oklahoma, 1996.

First published in 1976, Cary's personal account of life among the "Gower Gulch Cowboys" of early Hollywood (she was child star "Baby Peggy") is an engaging memoir of the real-life wranglers and cowhands who brought their experience into theaters around the world. They didn't need direction to do for the cameras what they'd been doing all their lives.

Cawelti, John G. *The Six-Gun Mystique.* Bowling Green: Bowling Green University, 1970.

An excellent work of scholarship, applying overdue respect to an often-maligned genre.

Durham, Philip, and Everett L. Jones. *The Western Story: Fact, Fiction, and Myth.* New York: Harcourt Brace Jovanovich, 1975.

Another respectful approach to a subject deeply ingrained in the American national character.

Emmert, Scott D. *Loaded Fictions: Social Critique in the 20th Century Western.* Moscow, Idaho: University of Idaho, 1996.

The further in time we drift from the history of the westward expansion, the more thoughtful studies of the lore it inspired become. This is another prime example of that phenomenon.

Estleman, Loren D. *"Lonesome Dove:* Star Robert Duvall Says: It's Going to Be like a Western Godfather." Radnor, Pennsylvania: *TV Guide,* February 3–10, 1989.

Perhaps it's bad form to recommend one's own work, but the material I gathered during this assignment is still worth sharing. *Lonesome Dove* rescued both the western and the miniseries format. Stars and crew recount their experiences on the set and set forth their own thoughts on the production and the form itself, with enthusiasm and fascinating personal philosophy.

Estleman, Loren D. Notes and tape-recorded interviews (See above).

Estleman, Loren D. *The Wister Trace: Classic Novels of the American Frontier.* Ottawa, Ill.: Jameson, 1987.
I include this (and the reference below) for its comparison of some of the great westerns in print and their screen adaptations.

Estleman, Loren D. *The Wister Trace: Assaying Classic Western Fiction, Second Edition.* Norman, Oklahoma: University of Oklahoma Press, 2014.
In the nearly thirty years since the appearance of the first edition, some impressive writing careers sprang up, followed by a new wave of films based on their work. In addition, significant contributors who were overlooked the first time found their way into this edition, for which I thank Charles E. "Chuck" Rankin and his wonderful staff at this great publishing house.

Everson, William K. *A Pictorial History of the Western Film.* Secaucus, NJ: Citadel, 1969.
Everson's was one of the first to explore western movies in detail. It's less scholarly than some, and a tad fan-centric, but

entertaining, accurate, and meticulously re-
searched.

Garfield, Brian. *Western Films: A Complete
Guide.* New York; Rawson, 1982.
  A page-turning delight. Garfield, a gifted
writer of westerns (*Wild Times,* etc.) and
thrillers (*Death Wish,* etc.), took on the
monumental task of reviewing nearly every
frontier drama ever shot from silent days to
date of publication, with copious stills for
illustration. You may not agree with his
sometimes acerbic opinions, but they're
based on actual screenings, which isn't
always true of books on movies.

Heide, Robert, and John Gilman. *Box-Office
Buckaroos: The Cowboy Hero from the Wild
West Show to the Silver Screen.* New York:
Abbeville, 1982.
  From Buffalo Bill Cody to "Cowboy
Mickey" Mouse, Heide and Gilman trace
the evolution of the western's popularity,
with information on and photographs of
stars, rodeo athletes, stuntmen (and
-women), and the proliferating market in
cowboy memorabilia. Educational and
scrumptious.

Jackson, Ronald. *Classic TV Westerns.* New

York: Citadel, 1994.

This press can always be relied upon to deliver accurate information in a matter-of-fact manner, but never stuffily, and always avoiding the "gee-whiz" factor frequently found in the literature of the performing arts, particularly where westerns are involved. This entry has all of the good qualities and is tasty besides.

Joyner, C. Courtney. *The Westerners: Interviews with Actors, Directors, Writers and Producers.* Jefferson, North Carolina: McFarland, 2009.

This one delivers on its subtitle. Its emphasis on gifted character actors like Jack Elam and Warren Oates, veteran leading ladies such as Virginia Mayo, writers and producers Andrew J. Fenady *(The Rebel)* and Elmore Leonard *(Hombre)* treats us to modest and open appraisals of their lives in hundreds of dusty locations and the stars with whom they shared experiences.

Knowles, Thomas W., and Joe R. Lansdale. *Wild West Show!* New York: Random House, 1994.

Dozens of western writers celebrate the West in print and on-screen, offering recollections from their personal experiences and captivating facts and trivia on history's most popular subject.

Moore, Clayton, with Frank Thompson. *I Was That Masked Man.* Lanham: Taylor Trade, 1998.

Just as Johnny Weissmuller will always be *the* Tarzan to many, there is no other Lone Ranger to my generation (and those that followed). TV's original portrayer of the character that began on WXYZ radio in Detroit provides an affectionate and whimsical account of his years aboard "the fiery horse Silver" alongside Tonto, his faithful Indian companion (played by Jay Silverheels, an authentic Mohawk). A real page-turner, written by a man every bit as honorable and self-effacing as the hero he played.

Place, J.A. *The Western Films of John Ford.* New York: Citadel, 1974.

Although he directed other types of films (*The Informer* and *The Quiet Man* alone would have made his reputation), Ford's name will always be synonymous with the western, and forever linked with John Wayne, his most frequent collaborator. Citadel's star-by-star and director-by-director guides are thorough and invaluable to anyone who writes about the movies (and beloved of anyone who watches them on a regular basis).

Savage, William W., Jr. *The Cowboy Hero: His Image in American History and Culture.* Norman: University of Oklahoma, 1979.
    Yet another serious study of a subject considered sub-intellectual for far too long. Savage plumbs the depths of the New World's sole mythos on the page, on celluloid, and in the collective consciousness.

Thomas, Tony. *The West that Never Was: Hollywood's Vision of the Cowboys and Gunfighters.* New York: Citadel, 1989.
    Again, Citadel brings its no-nonsense approach, with crucial details on plot, casts, crews, and release dates.

Tuska, Jon. *The Filming of the West.* Garden City: Doubleday, 1976.
    A tome, this, with enormously absorbing insight into the earliest westerns as well as the development of the movie genre into the seventh decade of the twentieth century.

Walsh, Margaret. *The American West: Visions and Revisions.* New York: Cambridge, 2005.
    Such thought-provoking studies are ap-

pearing more and more frequently, which
suggests that while the western's general
popularity has declined, interest in it as a
singular American feature continues to in-
crease.

Wright, Will. *Sixguns & Society: A Structural
Study of the Western.* Berkeley and Los
Angeles: University of California, 1975.
　See above.

DOCUMENTARIES

Action Heroes of the Wild West (1992, Good-Times). Compiled by Sandy Oliveri, produced by Film Shows, Inc.

Another of those smash-ups of in-public-domain trailers strung together in faded, unremastered condition, but rousing, and a crash course on the careers of Ken Maynard, Gene Autry, Johnny Mack Brown, Roy Rogers, Tim Holt, Tex Ritter and many more idols of the B western.

The American West of John Ford (1999, Front Row). Directed by Denis Saunders, written by David H. Vowell.

A thoughtful feature on a brilliant and difficult artist. Ford was almost paranoically cantankerous about any attempt to find "deeper meaning" in his work; but through interviews with those who knew him and excerpts of his western oeuvre, it comes to light.

Buffalo Bill's Wild West Show (undated, Old Army).

William Cody would object to that "show" in the title. He always called his venture simply "Buffalo Bill's Wild West," and referred to it as an "exhibition." However, this video contains precious footage on his early excursions onto the screen. It's all we have of the enterprise that invented the myth of the Old West in action. (Try to overlook the host's snarky commentary, inspired by that threadbare "Mystery Science Theater" approach to bad sci-fi films.)

Hollywood (1980, Thames Television). "Out West." Written, produced, and directed by Kevin Brownlow and David Gill.

I keep praying this priceless and enthralling series on silent films will be released on DVD; my pirated tapes are growing weary. Brownlow and Gill, film archivists who inspired the creation of Valentino, presented beautifully remastered footage of surviving silents, and assembled this project when many of the stars, directors, and crew members were still alive and available for interviews.

FILMOGRAPHY

1. The Classics.

Alias Jesse James. Directed by Norman McLeod, starring Bob Hope, Rhonda Fleming, Wendell Corey, Jim Davis, Gloria Talbott, Will Wright, Mike Mazurki, Sid Melton, Jack Lambert, Glenn Strange, George E. Stone, Iron Eyes Cody. United Artists, 1959.

Woody Allen has acknowledged Hope's influence on his comedic persona: the perennial coward who blunders his way into valor. A funny scene with a gila and a rattlesnake is a highlight, but it's trumped by the gunfight at the climax, with icons Hugh O'Brian (Wyatt Earp), Clayton Moore (The Lone Ranger), Jay Silverheels (Tonto), Gary Cooper and Gene Autry (themselves), Gail Davis (Annie Oakley), James Arness (Matt Dillon), and Fess Parker (Davy Crockett) walking on to dispatch the James gang. Roy Rogers plugs one, then says, "Happy trails to *you.*"

The Covered Wagon. Directed by James Cruze, starring J. Warren Kerrigan, Lois Wilson, Alan Hale, Ernest Torrence. Paramount, 1923.

The plot was ancient even then: a love triangle, Indian raids, et al.; and the silent acting is no great shakes, but the photography is stunning, and the extras, all sons and daughters of authentic pioneers, are worth watching because they go about the business of bedding down and hitching up their Conestogas just as their parents did, no direction needed. You rarely see history — as opposed to historical fiction — in motion.

Cowboy and the Senorita. Directed by Joseph Kane, starring Roy Rogers, Mary Lee, Dale Evans, John Hubbard, Guinn "Big Boy" Williams, Fuzzy Knight, Dorothy Christy, Lucien Littlefield, Hal Taliaferro, Bob Nolan and the Sons of the Pioneers. Republic, 1944.

The story, about a villain trying to cheat the girl out of the goldmine she's inherited, is older than Laurel and Hardy's *Way Out West* (whose musical interlude was superior to the production numbers seen here); but it's worth watching for the first teaming of Rogers and Evans. As with Bogie and Bacall in *To Have and Have Not,* they fall in love before our eyes.

In Old Santa Fe. Directed by David Howard, starring Ken Maynard, Gene Autry, Lester "Smiley" Burnette, Evalyn Knapp, George "Gabby" Hayes, H.B. Warner, Kenneth Thompson, Wheeler Oakman. Republic, 1934.

Although it may be stretching things to call it a classic, this bizarre story involving stagecoach robberies on a modern dude ranch is an important artifact: the transition of Maynard's era-bridging western career into Autry's as a "singin' cowboy," with Burnette and Hayes creating the template for the comic-relief sidekick.

Once Upon a Time in the West. Directed by Sergio Leone, starring Charles Bronson, Henry Fonda, Claudia Cardinale, Jason Robards, Jack Elam, Woody Strode, Lionel Stander, Keenan Wynn. Paramount, 1968.

Leone practically invented the "spaghetti western," and despite almost universally bad reviews, restored visual authenticity to the western, stripping its icons of their glamour, and extending the *cinema verite* of the great Italian movies of the postwar period into the 1960s. Here, he boldly casts perennial heavy Bronson and hero Fonda against type, and fulfills in epic form the promise he showed in the trilogy *(The Good, the Bad, and the Ugly, A Fistful of Dollars, For a Few Dollars More)* that made Clint Eastwood a superstar. The climactic clash of themes — Fonda's snarling electric guitars, Bronson's haunting harmonica — seals the deal.

Ride the High Country. Directed by Sam Peckinpah, starring Joel McCrea, Randolph Scott, Mariette Hartley, Edgar Buchanan, John Anderson, R.G. Armstrong, Warren Oates, James Drury, L.Q. Jones, Ron Starr, John Davis Chandler. MGM, 1962.

I'm with Valentino: This is the greatest western ever filmed. It represents a watershed, as young Peckinpah waves a gentle farewell to the heroic frontiersmen represented by McCrea and Scott and ushers in the gritty, authentic types personified by his repertory cast of lowbrows Armstrong, Oates, Jones, Anderson, and Chandler. The finale, with the old-timers shot from ground level upward as they march into a straight-up showdown with the villainous brothers while the music swells, is towering.

Shane. Directed by George Stephens, starring Alan Ladd, Jean Arthur, Van Heflin, Brandon De Wilde, Jack Palance, Emile Meyer, Edgar Buchanan, Elisha Cook, Jr., Ben Johnson. Paramount, 1953.

Ladd's notorious lack of physical stature has led to many unfair slights against his acting. In the hands of a director who saw no reason to dissemble his height, he was as good as they came. The bleak muddy hamlet, and costumes straight out of a Frederic Remington painting, make this one of the first authentic-looking westerns since the earliest silents, and Stephens' decision to tell the story visually from the boy's point of view, replicating the narration in Jack Schaefer's novel, make the principal actors as gigantic as their characters. Highlight: rival gunslingers Ladd and Palance size each other up in silence while Heflin and the cattle baron discuss their differences.

Son of Paleface. Directed by Frank Tashlin, starring Bob Hope, Jane Russell, Roy Rogers, Bill Williams, Lloyd Corrigan, Jean Willes, Chester Conklin, Harry von Zell, Iron Eyes Cody, Paul E. Burns. Paramount, 1952.

It's funnier even than *Paleface,* its predecessor. One highlight: Rogers says farewell, rearing the great horse Trigger; tenderfoot Hope returns the gesture, tilting his Model T touring car up onto its rear tires.

Stagecoach. Directed by John Ford, starring John Wayne, Claire Trevor, John Carradine, Andy Devine, Thomas Mitchell, George Bancroft, Donald Meek, Berton Churchill, Tim Holt. Warner Brothers, 1939.

The granddaddy of them all, rescuing the western just when critics predicted it had reached its saturation point and the first epic outdoor drama of the sound era. Every member of the ensemble cast has at least one honey of a scene, and from the moment the Duke made his explosive entrance, the world had a new star.

2. Tributes and Satires

Blazing Saddles. Directed by Mel Brooks, starring Cleavon Little, Gene Wilder, Madeline Kahn, Mel Brooks, Slim Pickens, Harvey Korman, David Huddleston. Warner Brothers, 1974.

The *Stagecoach* of cinematic spoofs, zany Brooks's opus hits on all the cliches and turns them on their heads. In scope and approach, the feature's main target seems to be the slick, big-budget 1940s westerns starring Errol Flynn. Kahn stands out in a brilliant cast, taking off on Marlene Dietrich's saloon-girl hellcat in *Destry Rides Again.*

City Slickers. Directed by Ron Underwood, starring Billy Crystal, Daniel Stern, Bruno Kirby, Patricia Wettig, Helen Slater, Josh Mostel, Davis Paymer. Columbia, 1991.

Jack Palance, in a (slightly) kinder, gentler take on his killer in *Shane,* won an Oscar for his role as a weathered trail boss in this clever send-up of every cattle-driving movie ever made. Crystal, Stern, and Kirby learn something about life in middle-age during a modern-day attempt to recapture the romance of the range. (*Viva* the "Yee-ha" scene!)

Hearts of the West. Directed by Howard Zieff, starring Jeff Bridges, Blythe Danner, Alan Arkin, Andy Griffith, Donald Pleasence, Burton Gilliam, Matt Clark, Marie Windsor, Richard B. Shull, Anthony James. MGM, 1975.

This is a charming recreation of on-set antics during the heyday of the "three-day oater" of the 1930s. Would-be screenwriter Bridges winds up a stuntman, then a B western star. It's uneven, but worth searching for.

Rustlers' Rhapsody. Directed by Hugh Wilson, starring Tom Berenger, G.W. Bailey, Marilu Henner, Andy Griffith, Fernando Rey, Sela Ward, Patrick Wayne. Paramount, 1985.

The critics dismissed this as a tepid *Blazing Saddles* wannabe, but they missed the point. It's an almost metaphysical meshing of the Roy Rogers/Gene Autry–style squeaky-clean oater and the genuine Old West. Griffith is amusingly cast against type as the villainous rancher, who accepting Berenger's assertion that the good guy always wins, hires Wayne (the Duke's handsome son) to challenge Berenger over which of them is *really* the good guy. Bailey's the comical sidekick, and there's a clever tongue-in-cheek scene during which Berenger practices his marksmanship, shooting guns out of targets shaped like hands! (Typical line, delivered in a tough-guy saloon: "I'll have a warm glass of gin with a human hair in it.")

Silverado. Directed by Lawrence Kasdan, starring Kevin Kline, Scott Glenn, Kevin Costner, Danny Glover, John Cleese, Rosanna Arquette, Brian Dennehy, Linda Hunt, Jeff Goldblum. Columbia, 1985.

As *Ride the High Country* is a crossover between old-time western and new, *Sil-*

verado is a hybrid: part tribute to the razzle-dazzle of the genre's heyday, part rousing western in its own right. Highlights include Costner's pure Hollywood fast-draw pyrotechnics and Dennehy, who walks away with everything but the sagebrush. There are perhaps one too many subplots for easy comprehension; but I wouldn't want to pick which one to throw out. This is a gem that gets brighter with each viewing.

IRIS OUT

What we are as a people, and what we like to think we are, say the same thing about us. Western culture is defined by the culture of the western. It's been estimated that westerns comprise ninety percent of all the films ever shot. However you feel about the winning (or losing) of the frontier, whatever your politics as regards the historical roles of men, women, government, the army, the indigenous peoples of America, their fates, and how they're portrayed, this much is true: If you don't like westerns, you don't like movies.

— Loren D. Estleman

ABOUT THE AUTHOR

Loren D. Estleman has written three previous Valentino film murder mysteries, *Frames, Alone,* and *Alive!,* and more than seventy books all told. Winner of four Shamus Awards, five Spur Awards, and three Western Heritage Awards, he lives in central Michigan with his wife, Deborah Morgan.

www.lorenestleman.com

The employees of Thorndike Press hope you have enjoyed this Large Print book. All our Thorndike, Wheeler, and Kennebec Large Print titles are designed for easy reading, and all our books are made to last. Other Thorndike Press Large Print books are available at your library, through selected bookstores, or directly from us.

For information about titles, please call:
  (800) 223-1244

or visit our Web site at:
  http://gale.cengage.com/thorndike

To share your comments, please write:
  Publisher
  Thorndike Press
  10 Water St., Suite 310
  Waterville, ME 04901